POUR DECISIONS

THE GIRL POWER ROMANCE COLLECTION

DENISE WELLS

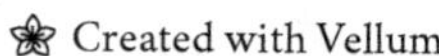 Created with Vellum

For the 50B Girls

Wine is win with an 'e' at the end.

— UNKNOWN

STANDALONES

The One I Can't Have, a steamy age-gap novella in **AB Worlds Age-Gap series**

The Three Way, a steamy novella in the **AB Worlds Valentine's Day Series**

Forever Wicked, a steamy novella in the **AB Worlds Halloween Party Series**

Summer Shivers, a romantic thriller in the **Summers in Seaside Collection**

Overdrive, a steamy enemies to lovers romance **in KB WORLDS - DRIVEN COLLECTION**

Pour Decisions, a romantic comedy novella in the **Girl Power Collection**

How to Ruin Your Ex's Wedding, a steamy romantic comedy

I Heart Mason Cartwright, a steamy romantic comedy

Love Off The Rocks, a romantic comedy short

Rebel without a Claus, a steamy, gay romantic short

Breaking Dylan, a coming of age story

AGENTS AND ASSASSINS TRILOGY

Fearless - Book One, a steamy romantic thriller

Careless - Book Two, a steamy romantic thriller

Ruthless - Book Three, a steamy romantic thriller

SAN SOLOMAN

Keeping Kat, a steamy second-chance firefighter romance

Romancing Remi, a steamy enemies to lovers romance

Loving Lexie, a steamy cowboy enemies to lovers romance

Seducing Sadie, a steamy firefighter romance

Trusting Tenley, an emotional second-chance at love romance

ANTHOLOGIES

High EX-Pectations, a romantic comedy short in the **Imperfect Date Anthology**

CAUGHT UNDER THE MISTLETOE - A Holiday Affair to Remember, a romantic comedy holiday short

STORYBOOK PUB CHRISTMAS WISHES - Mistle Oh-No, a romantic comedy holiday short

STORYBOOK PUB - Breezy Like Sunday Morning, a romantic comedy short

LIMITED RELEASES

GIRLS JUST WANNA HAVE FUNDAMENTAL RIGHTS - Charity Anthology

SEEDS OF LOVE A Charity Romance Anthology to benefit Ukraine - Charity Anthology

HOT AS F$#K SUMMER ROMANCE ANTHOLOGY - SULTRY SUMMER NIGHTS

LOCKED AND LOVED: An Isolated Romance Collection

SUMMER WITH YOU: Summer Shorts Collection

JUST A LICK Collection

LOVE LETTERS Collection

STOCKING STUFFERS Anthology

INTRODUCTION

I've been preparing for this day for years. The biggest wine competition of my career. And I plan to win.

My wine? Sublime.

My presentation? On point.

My outfit? Hand-picked by my fabulous BFF with fantastic fashion sense.

Nothing has been left to chance—I'm ready to crush my competition. No pun intended.

The thing is, that judge over there? I'm pretty sure he's the stranger whose bed I crawled out of this morning.

POUR DECISIONS

My eyes have a hard time opening. Last night's mascara holds my lashes together, making them stick like glue. I use my fingers to pry open the right, blinking rapidly to adjust to the light. It's dim, but still an intrusion from the black void of a moment ago. My head raises and my left eye mimics the right. My vision blurred and hazy. A sea of white surrounds me, accompanied by the faint smell of sex, sweat, and bleach.

I'm not good with mornings. I don't like them; they don't like me. As though in testament to such, my stomach protests as I sit up slowly. Could be that its morning, could also result from too much alcohol and not enough food last night. My head spins as I take in the surrounding room. I'm in a hotel room, that much I remember. It's a nice one, spacious and well furnished. One of those with separate bedroom and living room areas. A ceiling fan rotates above my head. I can't recall ever seeing a ceiling fan in a hotel bedroom before.

Blackout curtains cover the window while the faint hum of the air conditioning dances around my ears. A quick peek under the sheets shows my naked body glaring back at me while snippets of last night's festivities pepper through my mind. My girlfriend's and I venturing out to the Villa Royale hotel for drinks. What started as a low-key happy hour stretched into four, then five. Or was it six?

Dancing. Oh god, so much dancing my legs ache.

I'd gotten word early afternoon about my nomination for the West Coast Winemaker's Association (WCWA) Innovation Competition (WCWAIC). My friends Tess and Megan thought it would be a good idea to take me out for drinks and we came to the same hotel that is hosting the WCWAIC starting tonight. My face grins at the memories, my body stretches languorously, and my throat groans at how good it feels. All the parts working independently, yet simultaneously, while—

Oh. Wait.

My legs aren't the only part of me that aches.

I trail my fingers down between my legs and push gently at the sore, swollen tissue, remembering how thoroughly and completely that delicious man fucked me last night. Multiple times if the condom wrappers on the nightstand are any sign.

Wait again.

The man.

I glance to the other side of the bed, relieved to find it empty. My sleep-addled brain finally catching up to the fact that the only light in the room is filtering through the cracked bathroom door, where the shower is running. And all the pieces come together in a linear fashion.

The competition.

My nomination.

Tess, Megan, and me celebrating.

Copious amounts of drinks.

The gorgeous guy.

All that dancing.

Fantastic sex.

Aw, fuck!

I need to go now before the guy gets out of the shower and we have to do that awkward morning after thing that everyone talks about. Where you don't know if you should go to breakfast, maybe have sex again, trade numbers, or avert your eyes and go your separate ways. Not that I would know. This is my first one-night stand ever. But I've heard enough stories to be frightened.

I scramble from the bed and begin the hunt for my clothes. The room isn't cluttered, far from it, but I'm still having a hard time identifying things. I grab my fishnet stockings and try to pull them on while standing.

Oh, they're ripped.

Wow, really ripped.

Especially in the crotch.

Nicely done, Morgan.

I mentally pat myself on the back, before realizing I didn't need them on anyway. What better way to make the proverbial walk of shame look even more embarrassing than by wearing the ripped stockings from the night before

I shove them along with my bra into my purse. Searching for my underwear while trying to zip the back of my dress at the same time. Right arm over my right shoulder, left arm bent behind my lower back and moving up from the bottom. Both trying in vain to reach the zipper pull or each other. Clearly, dresses were designed by sadist contortionists with no concern for how normal people dress in short amounts of time or otherwise.

Grabbing my shoes and purse in one hand, all the while holding the front of my dress to my chest, I quietly slip out the door into the hallway. Then toe on my shoes as I hit the elevator call button and continue to try unsuccessfully to zip my dress. The telltale ding signals the elevator car and the doors open to reveal a tall blonde woman in gym clothes, toweling non-existent sweat off her face, just as I'm pushing my heel into my shoe.

I nod my head as I enter, and give her a small smile, trying to pretend everything is normal. My dress isn't half hanging off my body, and I'm not—

OHMIGOD!

The reflection in the mirrored walls of the elevator car show someone who can't possibly be me. I mean, it's my dress, but no way is that nest of tangles and disarray my hair. And the raccoon eyed face with streaked eye makeup belongs to a stranger.

I can't help but gasp once I see myself. My free hand flies to my hair as I attempt to pat it down before licking my finger and running it under my eyes to get the smudge under control.

"Crazy night, huh?" the girl asks. She looks nice when she smiles at me.

"You have no idea." I smile back, a feeling of camaraderie developing, as though we're sharing in a sisterhood of sorts.

"Want me to zip your dress?"

"Oh, god, would you," I breathe. "Thank you so much." I turn my back to her, shivering slightly as her icy hands graze my skin.

"Looks like you had a good time." She gestures to my neck.

I lean in closer to the mirror, inspecting the number of hickeys on my neck.

My first one-night stand.

My first hickey on other parts of my body that aren't my neck.

"I did." I smile, pivoting to face the front. A flyer announcing the WCWAIC competition hangs from a bulletin box above the button controls and snags my attention. My heart does a little flip knowing that starting tonight, I'll be a part of that. And a competition like this one, where innovations in the wine industry are judged and awarded, could make a career for someone as small-time as me.

The car stops and the doors open, I make my way out to the lobby. Feeling proud for stepping out of my comfort zone and doing something so ordinarily out of character. Both in submitting to the competition and in a one-night stand.

"Bye," I say to the girl as we part ways; she in the direction of the juice bar and me toward the exit. But as proud as I may feel in that moment, I still wait until I'm a block away before pulling up an app and ordering a car to come and take me home.

2

I pull up the messages on my phone to send a text to my best friend, Tess, and see all the pictures that she and Megan sent me the night before. Dozens of pictures of me on the dance floor with the guy from the hotel. And almost every single one they took is flattering. If it weren't for the fact the girl in the photos is wearing the same dress I am, I might not believe it's me.

This girl looks . . . hot.

Confident.

Sexy.

I'm not any of those things in my everyday life. Look up shy, mousy, and wallflower with social anxiety in the dictionary and there I will be. Which often makes me wonder how different my life would be if I were confident and sexy. Would I have a boyfriend? A better career? Might I have finally moved out of my mom and grandma's house to live on my own?

Cause none of those things are true now.

I'm working on the career part though. This award will help that along. If I win, that is.

Tess' words from last night ring through my mind.

When.

Not *if.*

When I win this competition, the recognition will help to further my career. The WCWAIC award is for showing innovation in wine making and selling techniques. Coming up with something that benefits the end user, i.e. the wine drinker, in a way that's not been done before. It's rare that a competition like this comes up, where the primary goal isn't focused on something more traditional, like "Best Cabernet Sauvignon" or something along those lines. There's just this one for the west coast, and then I think one of the big wine magazines has a national one.

Winning should mean more sales, which means more money, which is all I need to get a place of my own. While I may love my mom and grandmother, I don't need to be living with them any longer. I'm going to be thirty years old next year, I should have been out of their house six years ago. But they live where my grapevines live and I really love my vines.

I flip through more of the pictures with me and the guy who is so totally out of my league. As he kisses my neck, grabs my hips, laughs at whatever I'm saying. This girl has him captivated. How did I do it?

I dial Tess, hoping she's awake.

"Toot, toot, and beep, beep," she answers in a sing-song voice.

"What?" I ask, laughing.

"Bad girl. Talking 'bout the bad girl, yeah," she sings the Donna Summer song from seventies into the phone.

"I am not a bad girl, take it back!"

"I will not take it back. Last night was awesome! I've never seen you cut loose like that. You were having so much fun! Did you spend the night with him? Was the sex good? What did he say this morning? Did you exchange numbers? Are you doing the LYFT of shame home right now? Are you going to see him again?" She rattles off questions.

"Um, let me see." I tap my finger on my lips, pretending to think, even though she can't see me. "Yes. Yes. Nothing. No. Yes. And I doubt it."

"Nooo! Why?"

"Which of those responses are you asking why to?"

"Exchanging numbers. Seeing him again. Did you say anything to him?"

"No! I snuck out while he was in the shower."

"Morgan!"

"Tess!"

"Come on. Really? This has got to be your first one-stand in—"

"Ever," I interrupt.

"No," she gasps.

"Yes," I affirm, nodding.

She's silent for a moment. "I guess you're right. Well then, all the more reason why you should have embraced it. Jumped in the shower with him. Left your number in his wallet, a lipstick print on his boxers."

"I don't think so," I say.

"Spoil sport. Fine, let's get back to the sex then. You said it was good?"

"Better than," I whisper into the phone. I catch the LYFT driver's eye in the rear-view mirror and turn my head to the side, covering my mouth with my other hand. "Mind blowing." I lower my voice, not wanting him to hear.

"What?"

"Mind blowing. Like what we see in movies," I mumble.

"You guys watched a movie? Like porn?"

"No," I sigh. "I said like what we see in movies."

"Wow, like porn movies?"

"No, just normal movies. Or, I don't know, maybe porn," I giggle. This time when the driver looks back at me through the mirror, I meet his gaze and stare hard. Screw him for listening in. It's my conversation, not his. And it's private. Though, I probably shouldn't be having it in *his* car then, but whatever.

"I knew the sex would be great. He was so good looking!" Tess enthuses.

"Is that all it takes?"

"Pretty much. The better looking they are, the more sex they've had. And the more sex they've had, the better they are at it."

"What about that whole *average-guys-try-harder-in-bed* theory you had before?"

"Morgan, let's face it, anytime you get the opportunity to sleep with a hot guy over an average guy, you need to take the hot one. You never know when you'll get a chance again."

"Gee, thanks. You're quite the ego booster this morning."

"Oh, you know what I mean. Things like that don't happen to girls like us."

"Who are girls like us?"

"You know, average girls. We're cute, smart, successful, but there's nothing crazy extraordinary about us."

"And the ego boosts just keep coming," I say drily.

"Says the girl who just left the hot guy's bed."

"There is that," I say, tempted to blow on my fingernails, then shine them on the chest of my dress. Last night was like a coup for ordinary girls everywhere. Because the guy wasn't that drunk.

Riggs.

That's his first name. I didn't ask for his last. Even his name is sexy. I shiver at the memories of his hands roaming my body, his lips murmuring beautiful words, his eyes worshiping in their quest to see everything about me at once, yet still retain each detail. I should be on cloud nine after last night. And part of me is. But the part of me that didn't leave my number, or get his, and who snuck out while he was in the shower, that part of me knows I'll never change.

Always preferring the sidelines to center stage; the wall to the middle of the room; the backseat to the driver. Probably because my mom and grandmother are such drivers. There's not room enough for three of us in the same house. It's barely tolerable with the two of them. Which reminds me, I never did text my mom or grandma to say I wouldn't be home. Not that I have a curfew or anything, I'm a grown woman. But they worry when they don't know where I am or what I'm doing.

The driver turns onto the long dirt drive leading to our house. It's impressive when you don't realize that we're at the tiny square house to the west and not the multi-level chalet straight ahead. But that's a story for another time. Right now I've got to square my shoulders and prepare myself for the onslaught of questions the two pains in my neck are going to shower me with the minute I walk in the door.

"Hey, we're pulling up to the house, I'll call you back in a bit," I tell Tess.

"Later, bad girl."

I chuckle as I click to end the call and gather my purse, looking around to make sure I haven't left anything in the back seat. "I can tip through the app, right?" I ask the driver, even though I already know the answer to that.

"Yep," he nods once as he answers. It's a dumb question but I don't know of another way to let the driver know I plan to tip them. I don't want them driving away thinking I stiffed them until later when they get their paycheck or whatever and realize I did tip them. I mean, by then they may not even remember who I am or what day it was they drove me.

This way they have it on their mind, hopefully for a couple days, and then make the connection that I'm the girl who left the tip. Not that I'll ever see them again, but that's not the point. I want them to have the instant gratification of knowing I appreciated them and the service they provided, and that I plan to reward them financially.

I slip inside the front door as quietly as possible in hopes my mom and grandmother are still asleep or at the very least, preoccupied somewhere else. Which turns out to be futile. The familiar voices of the cohosts for a popular morning show are already echoing through the room, followed swiftly by the tenors of my mother and grandmother as they argue the points of the story that just aired. It won't matter what it was about, they will never see it from the same point of view. Even if one of them has to argue against their personal beliefs, they will over agreeing with the other. It's not something I understand or even try to.

"There you are!" my grandmother exclaims. "Come here right now, young lady."

I bow my head slightly and walk toward them, ready to be shamed for staying out all night without calling and then walking in looking like . . . well looking like a hot guy fucked me hard all night long.

"Morning, Grandma." I lean in to give her a kiss on the cheek. She smiles, but it's fast, and her face turns hard again.

I brace myself for whatever punishment is about to verbally rain down.

"You tell your mother that Tom Selleck's mustache is real. That man does not need to use a hair growth treatment on his face. He is all man. A real man. And real men can grow a proper mustache."

"It's too lush, Morgan. Look at it, no one has hair like that, facial or otherwise. He's got to be using extensions or some sort of potion. And it's definitely dyed."

I look back and forth between the two of them, not quite believing what I've walked into. They've rewound the program and have it paused on the man in question. I have to admit, his mustache looks lush, and very dark. Almost too dark. I squint at the screen, trying to see if anything looks amiss. But Tom Selleck looks just as he should, otherworldly handsome with all that thick, dark hair above his lip and atop his head.

Both women lean toward me from their chairs, waiting to hear my answer. As though this will be the time I will produce a tie breaker. I won't. I never have, and I probably never will.

"Hasn't it always looked like that?" I ask, trying to take the middle road. "Lush and full? Like, since he was young."

"Ha," they both say, even though I've proven neither point.

"Okay, well, I've got to go get ready for my day and plan out tonight." I wave over my shoulder as I head down the hall. Still wondering why no one said a word about my appearance or the fact that I was out all night.

3

I take a sip of my wine and continue to survey the crowded hotel ballroom before me. I wish I could say I'm in my element at a wine event, but social things aren't really my forte. Never mind that I am one of only five winemakers selected to compete for the WCWA award out of the hundreds who entered. To be one of the few who remain is an honor. I should be flying high on some simulated form of self-confidence but I'm not. Mostly because I'm just not that girl who can speak to total strangers with ease.

Except for last night when I talked to and flirted with Riggs. The funny part about that being, that girl on the dance floor wasn't really me either. At least it never has been before. Tess, Megan, and I did a video call debrief after I showered this morning and I filled them in on everything that happened after I went up to his hotel room last night. Well, mostly everything. Some of it I'm keeping to myself. Like how he told me I was sexy and beautiful. And how I drove him wild.

Compliments I never would have believed had it not been for his hard dick between us. Which I'm taking as proof positive that he was attracted to me. Which is why, as much as I tried not to, I spent most of the day looking at the pictures the girls took of Riggs and me. I'm happy they did, or I might never have believed it happened.

I try to use the memory to bolster my confidence now. This large ballroom filled with people from all facets of the wine industry. Winemakers, wine critics, grape growers, tasting room managers, cellar masters; and that doesn't include the wine store owners, distributors, PR people, marketing reps, wine journalists, and probably a dozen other occupations I'm not remembering to list.

They have the room decorated like a large barrel room. Two of the walls are covered with life-size photographs of racked barrels, and they scattered actual barrels about the room to use as tables to set your glass on or lean against. Plastic grape vines decorate each of the two walk-up bars in front of the glass doors leading to the patio. And the third wall is blanketed with the WCWA banner, underneath which are tables with assorted swag and marketing materials for the sponsors of tonight's cocktail party.

The event is meant to act as an icebreaker—bring us all together and ply us with wine before pitting us against one another tomorrow during the competition. At least pitting the five finalists against one another, I can't speak for how the rest of the entrants see it or feel.

Regardless, I need to be networking with some of the other competitors and introducing myself to all the judges. Not standing against the faux barrel wall polishing off my second glass of Sauvignon Blanc. The WCWAIC is a big event as far as someone like me is concerned. I own a boutique establishment focusing on hand-crafted botanically infused wines. Problem is, people often confuse the word infused with fortified and think I'm spiking the wine, like in making sherry or port.

I'm not.

I'm infusing the juice with fruits and herbs to alter the flavor profile during the aging process. It's more like what's done with an aromatized wine, like Vermouth. Though Vermouth is aromatized and fortified, so don't let that confuse you. My end goal is to make something fermented taste like something distilled—like a white wine with a similar flavor profile to vodka. It's an idea my dad had, and he passed away before he had the chance to do something about it. And so it's in his honor I try to see it through.

In my spare time, I like to see if I can recreate classic cocktails. At some point I hope to bottle and sell the "cocktails," but for now I make a little of money bottling my other wines and peddling them to local wine markets. It's not a lot, but it's enough to put food on the table. Between that and the juice I sell to the big wine maker who owns our property. But that's a story for another time.

I head over to the bar and get a refill on my wine, then make a concerted effort to congratulate each of my fellow competitors. There are five of us total, all small establishments with an annual production of five hundred cases or fewer. I see the wine maker from Bryn Hill and head over to congratulate him. Might as well get the worst over with first. Eat the big frog first, as the saying goes.

I tap him on the shoulder just as he's finishing a conversation with someone else. "Michael?" I ask.

He turns. "Morgan Anderson, how are you?" He looks me down and then up again, pausing at my chest and staying there. It's all I can do not to grab his chin and force his head upward until our eyes meet. I don't have large breasts. I don't even think they are that spectacular.

Though, Riggs thought they were perfect. One in each hand, his tongue flicking—

I shake my head to clear it as I feel my chest flush. The last thing I need is to be thinking about my one-night stand when I have to be focused on this event.

"You are looking lovely as always," Michael says to the "V" in the neckline of my dress.

What is it with men and their fascination with breasts?

Another thing I definitely do not understand. I mean, my dress isn't even too low cut, or particularly revealing. But he'll have his eyes focused on my chest for the bulk of our conversation. Michael and I have conversed before at the local WCWA chapter events, but apparently I'd forgotten how creepy he can be.

"I just wanted to congratulate you on your nomination," I tell him, holding out my hand to shake his.

He holds my hand too long for comfort, then drags his finger along my palm and up my wrist when I try to pull mine away. I barely repress the resulting shudder.

"May the best man win," he says, leaning toward me like he's going to—

Oh god, is he going to try to what? Hug me? Kiss me?

"I see *mmrhsmrh*, gotta go!" I mumble the words, since I haven't seen anyone I need to talk to and take off across the room to hide in the corner behind a large, fake ficus tree. Which I feel justified in doing and like a wuss at the same time.

First, Michael gives me the creeps. Second, I can't stand networking. Why do I have to talk to all these people? Or get to know them? I try to look at it like they are all potential customers, but let's face it, they aren't. My competitors aren't going to buy my product. Why would they? And most of the rest of the people here are looking for handouts. They just see the hundreds, if not thousands of bottles you produce and figure, what's one little freebie? But they don't take into account everything it took me to make that one bottle.

Time, effort, money, talent, discipline, sweat, tears, and luck.

Not to mention the things I have to pay out of pocket for: everything from labels, corks, caps, bottles, and barrels to vineyard workers, field equipment, lab tests, alcohol taxes, wine making equipment, climate controlled barrel storage, and more. And, while I'm on a rant, I really dislike having to be polite to people I don't like. (Read: Michael) How is it that of all these people here, he is the only one I know?

I've been in this industry for almost eight years, and he's the only person in the room that I've met before. It's my fault, I hardly ever go to the WCWA chapter meetings. And when I do, I sit in the back and leave right after. I pay dues for North American Wine Makers' Association, but I rarely attend their events or meetings either. This is one of the first wine related events I've been to in years. Proof positive you can't be successful in a customer facing business without facing people or customers.

I work myself into a state of agitation, annoyed when my hands start to shake. The iron hold of self-doubt and insecurity wrapping its way around my confidence and motivation like a vise. Get a grip, Morgan. These are people just like you. There is nothing special or different about them. They hold no power over you. But believing that and living it are two different things. It's why last night is such an anomaly, and one that I'm grateful to have photographic proof of, since it's never happening again.

I see a woman wearing a judge lanyard near me, and she's alone. I square my shoulders and head out from behind the plant to catch her before she talks to someone else.

"Hi, I don't think we've met. My name is Morgan Anderson, I'm with Morgan's Run. Obviously, hence the name. I mean, I didn't name it, my father did. I'm not the type to name my winery after myself. Not that there's anything wrong with that. Anyway, I just wanted to introduce myself and thank you for the opportunity." My words come out a little too fast and I don't stop to take a breath between words or sentences, so my chest is heaving slightly by the time I'm through.

"Nancy Challis, nice to meet you." She shakes my hand limply before dropping it.

"That's funny," I say before I can stop myself. "Your last name is one letter off from being Chablis. And you're in the wine industry."

She blinks.

A few times.

I want to cringe. Dig a hole and jump inside it. Run back to the corner and hide behind the fake ficus. I hate my inability to refrain from making stupid comments, which I start out by saying they are funny, when they really aren't. Especially when I first meet someone. Tess says it's cute and quirky. That it's my way of breaking the ice when meeting someone.

I disagree.

It appears Nancy Challis disagrees as well.

"Good luck with the competition," she says before turning to walk away.

Good luck?

Like, as in you're going to need it? Or is she just being polite? The funny thing is, for as shy and awkward as I am in a group, I'd probably ask her if I could figure out a way to do so without making myself look even worse.

Because for as shy and reserved and socially awkward as I am, I'm also persistent and stubborn with a tendency to over share. I know, try being in my head sometimes. It's confusing as hell. I can go from wallflower to in-your-face at the blink of an eye. But right now all I really want to do is go home, slip into my pj's and watch reruns of Project Runway.

I find the second judge in the crowd and make my way through the introductions, smiling like a fool and trying not to sound like a suck up. Fighting with myself every step of the way.

It's just a necessary evil, Morgan.

Find the other contestants and the one last judge and you can go home.

I follow my own advice and make it through meeting the rest of my competition without issue. Or at least without feeling like a total idiot. And the last person I spoke to even pointed me toward the remaining judge. I can either wait for him to finish talking to—ew—Michael; or I can interrupt their conversation and get it over with. Before I can decide, a tall blonde woman joins them and receives a pat on the ass from Michael. She preens at the judge, playfully slapping him on the arm as though she's flirting.

Well, good for her. And good for Michael, that may be the only way that he can win is if his date flirts with the judge. At least I hope that's his date whose ass he still has his hand on. I mentally pat myself on the back for the mental snub. Wishing I could say it to him aloud and in person.

Michael takes that moment to gesture toward me. I think. I turn around to see if anyone is behind me.

Nope.

It's me.

And oh shit.

I'm pretty sure the woman with him is the same one from this morning, who zipped my dress. What if she says something to the judge? Or to Michael? I mean, having a one-night stand isn't against the law, obviously. My personal life is my own. And it doesn't matter to the competition who I have sex with. I mean, unless it was a judge or another entrant.

I chuckle to myself, as I recall the two judges I've met and how preposterous it would be to sleep with either of them. Especially to win a competition.

Michael waves me over.

I meet the blonde woman's gaze. Yep, it's definitely the one from this morning. And there it is, that flash of recognition that crossed her face. She remembers me too.

Lovely.

Okay, no matter. I did nothing wrong. If anything, it's a tad embarrassing to be caught leaving a man's hotel room at the crack of dawn with your dress still unzipped. But it's not the end of the world, right? Plus, I'm living proof that a little embarrassment never killed anyone.

I heard toward the trio as Michael says something else to the judge; who takes a drink of his wine, turning toward me just as I approach. And promptly spits a fine mist of red wine across the bodice of my dress.

It's Riggs.

"Maggie?" he gasps.

"Riggs?"

"You two know each other?" Blondie asks.

"Her name is Morgan, not Maggie," Michael says. I'd almost forgotten I used my *bar name* last night. Not that I go out much, but Tess and Megan both have them, so we came up with one for me as well. And that's how I introduced myself to Riggs.

"I . . . uh . . . we . . ." I start, not knowing what to say. Looking down instead at my chest, trying to brush away the already absorbed splatters of wine across the light blue material.

"Yes. Well, not intimately," Riggs says, heat flares in his eyes as though he's remembering last night. "Er, I mean, well. Long, that is. We haven't known each other long. We met last night. And oh, god, I'm so sorry." He takes the cocktail napkin from under his glass and dabs at my chest. The gesture both familiar and awkward.

"Briefly," I add. "I mean, not brief, it wasn't brief. It was long. But, uh, yeah, my name is Morgan. Haha." My face turns hot, I can feel the color traveling from my diaphragm up my chest and face all the way to my hairline. I should be the color of a cooked lobster about now. Or someone who is very sunburned. Or—

"Huh, I don't know where I got that your name was *Maggie*," Riggs grits his teeth at the last word, glaring at me.

I wave him off. "No biggie, happens all the time. Morgan, Maggie, so close," I squeak.

"So, you two don't know each other?" Blondie butts in.

"No," I say at the same time Riggs says, "Yes." Then we reverse, sounding like a *Laurel and Hardy* bit.

"Can I speak to you a moment?" Riggs asks.

"Sure," I say nervously, spreading my arms to show anywhere is good.

He takes my upper arm in his hand and pulls me alongside him. A zing travels down my body to my toes. I look back to Blondie and Michael, not for help, but to see how they are gauging the situation. Both are glaring.

Great.

Riggs doesn't stop until we are all the way across the room near the exit doors and down the hall that leads to the restroom. He spins me by my arm to face him. "*You're* Morgan Anderson?" His face is furious. I may not know him well, but I know people well enough to know he's pissed.

"*You're* judge number three?" I ask, working my way toward equally pissed. Not so pissed that I can't drink him in. My memory of him is not so crisp, thank god for the photos, or I may have forgotten just how attractive he is.

"Which wouldn't have mattered had I known your actual name." His eyes bounce back and forth between mine.

"Of course it would matter. How would it not?"

"Because last night never would have happened if I knew who you were," he says, his face softening. If it weren't for the fact that his jaw was so visibly tense I may have missed it. But I definitely would not have missed the regret in his eyes. Regret over not being able to pursue a romantic relationship further? Or maybe not knowing my actual name? For all I know, it's regret over sleeping with me at all.

"Well, maybe it never would have happened if I knew who *you* were," I throw back at him.

"We're saying the same thing," he says, looking off to the side, running his fingers through that soft sandy blond hair of his. The same hair that I ran my own fingers through last night while he buried his head between my—

"No one can know about this," he says, pulling me further into the hall.

"I know that. *I'm* not about to tell anyone."

"I'm certainly not going to tell anyone," he hisses.

"Good."

"Good," he mimics. His eyes dart around over my head as though he wants to make sure no one is watching. The door to the restroom opens, and he turns toward the wall, eyes downcast, masking his face in the shadows until they pass by.

Riggs angles back to face me. His gaze slowly travels up my body, crinkling his nose as he pauses at my chest before meeting my eyes.

He crinkles his nose.

Like he's disgusted by what he sees.

Something inside me snaps. Before I can stop myself, the words are out, "Are you embarrassed by me?" I can't help my gut reaction. I mean, you've seen him. And you've seen me. Do the math.

His gaze jerks back to mine. "What?"

"Are you embarrassed by me?" I'm surprised I'm asking again. But that doesn't stop me from doing it. I need him to recant all the wonderful things he said to me last night so I can go on with my life void of romantic daydreams and visions of a handsome prince on a white horse. Back to my day-to-day living that doesn't include sexy one-night stands who worship my body for hours on end.

"No, I'm not embarrassed by you. Jesus, Mag . . . Morgan. Why would you think that? Especially after last night? I mean, I know it was only one night, but I thought we had a connection."

"Why me?" I ask.

"Why you, what?"

"Why did you ask me to dance last night? Out of all the girls at the bar, what was it about me that made you approach?"

"Shit, I don't know. You looked happy, and like you were having fun, I liked your smile. And you looked really hot in that dress."

He's right, I did look hot in that dress.

Still. . .

"Hey, bud, we're gonna head out. Catch you later?" I look up to see Michael and Blondie beside us. Michael has his hand on Riggs' shoulder. Like they're friends. Blondie is looking at me curiously; part intrigue and part distaste. God, they didn't hear anything we said, did they?

"Yeah, man, I'll call you. Maybe we can do breakfast in the morning before the whole thing gets started or something," Riggs says back, giving Michael one of those one-armed guy hugs.

Michael turns to me. "Morgan, a pleasure as always," he says to my chest, taking a moment to drag his eyes along my entire body before making a sound eerily reminiscent of "Yum" then dragging Blondie by the hand after him as they exit the room

"You know Michael?" I ask.

"Yeah, we go way back. Why?"

"It all makes sense now," I tell him.

"What makes sense?"

"Why you picked me."

"I already told you why."

"You told me your excuse, your phony trumped up plan, but not your reason."

"What are you talking about?"

"You're setting me up so Michael can win the competition."

"What?" he asks, his face incredulous.

"You heard me."

"Are you nuts?"

"Are you?" Okay, not my finest comeback. But I'm incensed, beyond even. So much so, I can barely collect my thoughts.

"How would I be setting you up exactly?"

"By finding out my submission ideas and then telling Michael so he can sabotage me."

"Ah." He throws his arms in the air. "Well, nice work, Sherlock, you've caught me. Given we spent all night discussing your *ideas* and I know everything about your business now. If you'll excuse me I need to find Michael so I can tell him all about it."

"Just because it didn't work doesn't mean it wasn't your plan."

"You've got a screw loose, lady. I did nothing of the kind. I didn't even know who you were. Hell, I thought your name was Maggie until just a few minutes ago. And tonight was the first time I've seen Michael in years."

I have two choices here. Believe him or not. If I believe him, I risk last night being real. And what he said earlier about our having a connection being true. If I don't believe him, my life goes back to normal.

Not that anything was ever going to progress beyond one night anyway with Riggs. I mean just because I spent most of the day, okay all day, fantasizing about him doesn't mean he did the same with me.

"You know, when I got out of the shower this morning and saw that you were gone, I was upset. I'd been thinking we'd go for rounds five and six, maybe order in some breakfast, at the very least exchange last names and telephone numbers. But now I'm realizing I got off easy. I should be thankful you left. Because I gotta tell you, if it's the reality train you were looking to catch, that baby left the station a while ago and you definitely were not on it."

His chest heaves as he gets worked up. I can't help but remember how the muscles contracted under my palms when I took my turn on top. Or how good it felt under my cheek as I fell asleep after.

Then his words sink in.

That's like the tenth time he's called me crazy in this brief conversation. He hasn't seen anything yet.

"I'm reporting you." I point my finger at that same broad, heaving chest.

"To who?" He scoffs.

"To the WCWA board. You can't just go messing around with peoples' lives. It's unethical and immoral."

"If that's what you think is going on, then go right ahead. Don't come crying to me when they laugh you out of there for being ridiculous," he says.

"I am."

"Great."

"Great."

"It's Daley."

"What's Daley?" I ask.

"My last name," he says. "It's Daley. You know for when you report me for such unethical and immoral behavior. Better make sure you've got the right judge."

"This isn't a joke."

"I didn't say it was."

"I'm turning you in."

"Go right ahead."

"See ya." I turn and leave him standing there, off on my search to find a board member so I can turn him in.

Now that I'm on a mission, the crowd seems much smaller and more manageable. I make my way through a small gathering of people, tight smile pasted to my face, and zero in on Barbara Hershey, the president of the WCWA board.

Ha, that's makes two people here that I knew. Well, three if you count Riggs. But I'm not going to.

I tap her on the shoulder. "Barbara, it's so nice to see you again. May I borrow you a moment, I have something of great concern to discuss and I don't think it can wait any longer."

She faces me, looking down her nose. I never understood that phrase until now, but it is possible for tall people to look down their noses, literally, at shorter people. And also people who disgust them. As it seems—if her expression is any indication—I do to Barbara.

"Morgan, how fortuitous, I too have something to discuss with you. Shall we?" She motions toward the exit and begins walking in that direction, leaving me no choice but to follow her.

5

Barbara leads me down a narrow hall, away from the ballroom where the reception is, and stopping at a small conference room that is being used as an office for the WCWA staff.

She takes a seat at the head of the table and motions for me to take one at her side. Her hands fold on the table as she sits primly, waiting for me to get settled.

I jump right in. "Barbara, I—"

"Morgan," she interrupts. "I hope you know how seriously we take these competitions."

"Of course. In fact—"

She holds up one of her aged, boney fingers to stop me. Like I'm a child. Still, it works.

She continues. "Result tampering is one hundred percent against the rules."

How did she find out so fast? Maybe someone overheard Riggs and I and reported him already. Or maybe he's done it to every entrant except for Michael just to make sure Michael wins. Except he couldn't have slept with anyone else last night, I can attest to that.

Doesn't mean he didn't do it today, I suppose.

All day, even.

But with whom? All my competition is male.

He could be bisexual. Just because he slept with me doesn't mean he can't also sleep with men. Working his way through the entire entrant pool like the disgusting pig that he is. Which means he's had a lot of sex in the last day or so. Thank god we used condoms.

What an asshole.

To go to such extremes just to make sure your friend wins. And I can't believe Michael wouldn't rather win because of his talent and not cheating. I mean, he's a good winemaker. Not great, but definitely good. And his ideas are innovating. That should be enough for him. The award won't get him anything if he doesn't have the chutzpah to carry it through and deliver on what he promised.

At least they will both get what they deserve.

"—I'm sorry to tell you, you've been disqualified."

Wait.

What?

"You mean Riggs is disqualified?" I confirm.

"Well, no, we hadn't planned on that. So far, you're the only one with wrongdoings."

"Me?"

"Yes. Bribing a judge to win a competition is not okay." Her lips purse, the wrinkles surrounding them becoming more pronounced. Something I doubt she'd appreciate knowing.

"Whoa. Hold up. You think I bribed a judge?"

Barbara nods, her head moving, but her shellacked white hair stays perfectly in place. "Riggs Daley. And I think we both know I'm using the word bribe loosely."

She emphasizes the word loose with a second nod in my direction. As though I'm loose.

Ohmigod. They think I slept with Riggs to win the competition.

"Barbara, I think there's been a mistake," I start.

"No mistake, Morgan. We have an eyewitness who saw you come out of his room this morning in a state of undress."

"I wasn't undressed," I protest.

"Shoes off?" she asks.

I nod.

"Dress unzipped?" she adds.

I nod again.

Who could have seen me? That hallway was empty.

She leans back in her chair, as though she's rested her case and the jury can now find me guilty and sentence me to death by hanging.

"Okay, I was in a state of undress, as you put it. But I didn't know who he was before I slept with him."

"So you did have sexual relations with Riggs Daley?"

"Yes," I answer.

"But you claim to not know who he was."

"Right. I didn't."

"He gave you a false name?"

"No."

"I see. So he told you he was Riggs Daley, and you—"

"Riggs," I interrupt.

"That's what I said."

"No, I mean, he just said his name was Riggs. He didn't give me his last name."

Somehow she's able to look down her nose at me again, even though we're both sitting. It's remarkable how small I suddenly feel.

"You had sexual relations with a strange man in his hotel room without knowing his last name?" she asks.

When she says it like that, it sounds kind of bad. Not bad, like slutty, but bad like dangerous. Like I'd knowingly put myself in harm's way. Or maybe she means slutty, who knows?

"Yes, but—"

"Tell me, do you read the WCWA's publications that we send out via email?"

"Of course."

"So, you read the notification last week of a replacement judge by the name of Riggs Daley stepping in for Marcus Johnson?"

"No, I didn't."

"So you don't read the publications?"

"I do, I just didn't read that one."

"Convenient, since what are the chances there would be two men named Riggs staying here at this hotel at the same time as our competition?"

She's right.

Ohmigod, did I read it and I just don't remember? Or worse yet, did I read it and then tuck it away in the back of my subconscious, only to have it resurface last night in the form of the nudge I needed to go back to Riggs' hotel room with him? Did I seduce him to win the contest and I just don't realize it?

Maybe I really have lost my mind.

Or maybe I have an alternate personality who was trying to set it up so I'd win. Except I remember everything. And don't the other personalities usually not know what's going on. Oh, unless I'm the dominant one.

"Morgan?" Barbara interrupts my thoughts, which is probably a good thing, all considered, since I have a tendency to let my imagination go a little wild.

"Yes. Sorry. I spaced out for just a moment."

"Yes, well. I just wanted to say I wish you success with your future endeavors."

"Wait, Barbara, I think there's been a misunderstanding here."

"You didn't spend the night with Riggs Daley to win the competition?"

"No. Well, yes. I mean, I spent the night with him, but I swear I didn't know who he was before had. And he approached me, not the other way around. In fact, I think he's purposefully sabotaging the competition so that Michael Monroe can win."

"Why would you think that?" she asks.

"Well, they are friends for one."

Silence.

Making me feel the need to add more words to fill it.

"And I think he was trying to find out my plans so he could sabotage my entry."

"I see. And so what did you tell this stranger whose last name you did not know about your competition plans when you went back to his hotel room to have sexual relations?"

"Nothing."

"So how was he to gather the information necessary to sabotage you?"

"I don't know. This was his plan, not mine. I'm just saying it's way too convenient that he sought me out, of all the women in the bar, *and* that he's friends with Michael *and* he's the judge."

"All true," Barbara concedes. "But still not as convincing as you knowing who he was before going back to his room with him. I'm sorry, Morgan. But my decision has to be final."

"Someone is setting me up," I cry.

"Who?" She sighs. I'm pretty sure I see her eyes roll.

"Michael and Blondie. I saw her this morning in the elevator after I left Riggs' room. She zipped up my dress."

"I'm not sure who *Blondie* is, but you're saying she saw you coming out of Riggs' room and offered to zip up your dress."

"Yes."

"So you admit to everything except for your intention in sleeping with Riggs Daley?"

"Yes."

"Morgan, surely you can see this from my perspective? You claim to receive and read the email publications from WCWA. Yet somehow you missed the one announcing Riggs as a judge which featured his name and photograph. Then you meet a man named Riggs in a bar that is in the same hotel as the competition the day before the festivities are to begin."

She pauses a moment. I don't like where this is going. Not that it isn't true, it is. But the way she's describing it makes me sound way too guilty.

"You don't ask for his last name or his occupation before agreeing to go to his hotel room and spend the night with him. The next morning you're caught by someone you later find out is involved with your competition, and now suddenly they are out to get you."

Okay, I get how she thinks I'm guilty, but Michael is behind this, I'm sure of it.

"Barbara, I know how this must look, but I swear I'm telling the truth." I search her face for some semblance of acceptance but find nothing. Tears well in my eyes.

Don't cry. Don't cry. Don't cry.

"Rest assured we won't be pressing charges—"

"Charges?! For what? I haven't done anything wrong. This is ridiculous. You have to—"

"Result tampering is a serious offense."

"Ohmigod! They can arrest me for that?"

"Arrested? No. I mean we won't be bringing charges with the WCWA Board."

"Oh." I can't help the relief that floods my voice. Not that being censured by the WCWA Board isn't bad, it is. But somehow in my mind the dissolution of my career isn't as bad as the reneging of my freedom.

She cocks her head. "It will be quite some time before you are welcome back to one of our competitions, if ever again. You understand that, right?"

"I understand," I say. Even though I don't, not at all. Just somehow the relief in knowing I'm not being arrested by the police makes everything seem tame in comparison.

Barbara stands and exits the room, leaving me alone with my thoughts and tears. I know Michael is responsible for this. Somehow. And Riggs too. I hate them both. If I'm to find a silver lining here, I guess now I have the rest of the evening to plot my revenge.

6

I wake the next morning with no better plan than what I went to sleep with the night before. Which is nothing. No plan. Zero revenge plots to carry out. I'm a vengeance ignoramus.

I toyed with the idea of calling Tess and Megan about a million times through the night, but I didn't go through with that either. One, because I didn't want to admit they had disqualified me. And two, because I want to see if I can come up with something on my own. So far, the only thing I'm certain of is that I should have called Tess and Megan because me on my own can't come up with squat.

The doorbell rings, interrupting my musings.

I glance at my cell, it's not even nine o'clock in the morning. I listen for my mother or grandmother to answer before remembering that they planned to hit up the free pancake breakfast at the church this morning. We aren't devout, far from it. We're worse than that - the holy when its handy kind of crowd. And it's handy about four times a year. The pancake breakfast, Easter brunch, July Fourth picnic, and Christmas. Because god forbid we don't go to church on Christmas. No pun intended.

I glance at my reflection in the hall mirror on my way to the front door. If you take my reflection from yesterday, but remove all the makeup, that's me today. Still tired, with bags under my eyes, bed-head hair, and dried drool on my chin.

The knocking starts just as I'm reaching the door. I throw the lock and fling it open.

Riggs is standing on my front porch. Looking better than anyone has a right to at it's-too-early-for-visiting-o'clock.

I slam the door in his face and begin the retreat to my room.

He knocks again. "Morgan? Can I talk to you for just a second? Please?"

I pause.

I'm tempted. If for no other reason than to let him know how pathetic and disgusting I think he and his friends are.

So, I trudge back to the door and pull it open once more.

He smiles. "Thank you." Then hands me a to-go coffee cup and holds up a big pink box. "I brought coffee. And dough-nuts. A peace offering, if you will."

"What kind of donuts?"

"I got an assortment. From a place down the way about a mile."

He's talking about Wilson's Bakery. They have excellent donuts. I consider taking the box and slamming the door in his face again. Because it felt good to do it the first time. Instead, I open the door wider and let him in. "Come on in." I lead the way across the small room and gesture to the kitchen table.

He sets the box on the table. "Did I wake you?"

My eyes shut. My head bows. I forgot about my appearance. I take a deep breath and let it out in a huff, before remembering I haven't brushed my teeth either.

Kill me now.

Please.

I take a large drink of the coffee he brought, burning my tongue in the process. I swish the hot liquid around my mouth anyway to burn off the germs that cause morning breath. That works, right?

"No, you didn't wake me, I always look like this." I can't tell if he gets the sarcasm or not, so I just keep talking. "You know, you've got a lot of nerve coming here like this after what you did."

"I wanted to apologize."

"Good. You should. For what?"

"I found out what happened, that they disqualified you. I feel bad for whatever part I played in that."

"You mean the whole part you played in that, where you set it up with Michael?" I ask. "Is that the part you feel bad about?"

"I didn't set it up with Michael. I don't know where you got that idea from."

"I got it from the fact that it's the most logical explanation for what happened."

"Me and Micheal setting something up is the most logical explanation for you getting removed from the competition?"

"And an explanation for why you asked me to dance to begin with."

"Why do you have such a hard time accepting I was attracted to you?"

"Pfft." I gesture to myself then reach in the box to pull out a donut and take a large bite to further prove my point. Trying not to dwell on the fact he used the word *was.*

"Anyway, I wanted to see if I could make it up to you. Maybe by helping you find another competition to enter."

"I don't need you doing me any favors," I tell him, finishing the first donut and grabbing another. Any second now the sugar rush will kick in and I'll find the energy to throw him out.

"My god, you're difficult. I don't know why I even bothered." He throws his hands in the air and turns to leave.

I watch as he walks toward the front door, torn between wanting to stop him or eat some more donuts, then go back to bed.

"Riggs, wait," I say finally. "I'm sorry. I just . . . I don't know what my problem is. Give me a second, I'll be right back."

He hesitates.

"Please," I add, gesturing toward the table, hoping he takes the hint to sit back down, then rush down the hallway toward the bathroom. My hands going immediately to my hair, trying to smooth it down on the sides. When that doesn't work, I throw it up in a messy bun and leave it at that. I gargle with mouthwash, splash some water on my face, then at the last second throw on some mascara and lip-gloss.

Feeling moderately presentable, I head back to the dining room. Where Riggs, if my calculations are correct, is polishing off his fourth donut. I raise a brow and tilt my head toward the box.

He smiles sheepishly. "I was hungry. That's why I brought a dozen."

He's cute when he smiles. More than cute really, sexy would be a better descriptor. He makes my nether regions all tingly and excited.

I wave my hand in the air, dismissing my own unspoken admonition.

"Truce?" I offer my hand so we can shake on it. He smirks but takes it anyway.

"Truce," he confirms. "Now, will you listen to me when I tell you I didn't have some master plan with Michael to get you thrown out of the competition?"

I grab a donut from the box. "You can tell me whatever you want to now, the plan worked."

He looks at me, brows raised.

I still the hand bringing the donut to my mouth. "Okay, yes. I will listen."

"Good." He grabs another donut from the box. His fifth or sixth at this point. I want to ask how the donuts are a peace offering for me when he's eating them all, but I don't. Because what am I going to do with a dozen donuts outside of eat them? And if I eat a dozen donuts, even half a dozen, I'll hate myself.

Which is also what stops me from keeping this third donut in my hand. Instead, I put it back in the box. Then slip that same hand under my thigh to keep it restrained and take the coffee cup in my other to keep it busy while I wait.

And wait.

I smile in what I hope is an encouraging manner to show him he can begin talking at any time. Convince me of how he doesn't have some master plan with Michael to take me down. Only he just smiles in return in between bites of donut and sips of coffee.

"Well?" I ask when I can't take the silence any longer.

He looks confused. "Well, what?"

"Tell me how you didn't conspire against me to get me thrown out of the competition," I urge.

"I already did," he says.

"No, you didn't. All you did is tell me you didn't have some plan with Michael." I set my coffee down and lean across the table toward him. My face reddening with anger.

"Exactly."

"That's it? That's all you have to say about it?"

"What more is there to say?"

"I don't know, this is your issue, not mine."

"I'm not the one who is accusing you of something you didn't do."

"You also aren't the one who is convincing me you didn't do it."

"Look, either you believe me, or you don't."

I fold my arms across my chest and glare at him, letting my actions speak for me.

"Wow, okay." He stands while running a napkin across his lips, before tossing it back to the table. "I thought maybe we'd turned a corner, but I guess not."

I shrug in what I hope is a show of nonchalance. "You didn't even say anything."

"Oh, but I did. I told you I didn't do it. That should be enough."

I turn my head away from him and look down, purposefully avoiding his gaze. Because it's not enough. At least I don't think it is. And I don't know how to make it be enough, since it really should be. So, I trust the guy enough to go back to his hotel room with him telling no one where I'm going or finding out any information about him first. I spend the night with him. I let him into my house this morning when I'm home alone. Yet I refuse to take him at his word?

He pauses at the front door, like he's going to say something else, one hand on the knob with the door partially opened.

I wait, not knowing what I want, but still knowing I want something.

Instead of saying anything more, Riggs disappears out the door, closing it softly behind him.

I attempt to smother my sorrows with that third donut. When that doesn't work, I move on to a fourth.

7

"I'm sorry, could you repeat that please?" Tess says via video chat. "Because I could have sworn I just heard you say you let the man leave after all that."

"I won't repeat it because you know that's what I said, since that's what happened." I'm pacing while we talk. I like the routine of doing so in the small space of my bedroom. One. . . two. . . three. . . four. . . five. . . pivot and repeat.

"Why did you let him leave?"

"Did you not hear anything that I just said?"

"Yes, I did. And he told you he didn't do it."

"Of course he's going to say he didn't do it, otherwise he'll be in big trouble."

"How?" Tess asks.

"What do you mean *how*?"

"I mean how will he be in big trouble? What exactly is going to put him in trouble? He's already got you out of the competition? He's not getting into trouble with WCWA or he would have already. There's nothing else he needs to concern himself with."

She has a point.

"Well, he made me mad at him," I say.

"And he visited you first thing in the morning, *before* the competition, to bring you coffee and donuts, explain, and apologize."

She has a point with that too.

"So, what are you saying?" I ask dumbly.

"I'm saying, guilty people don't do that, so how the hell could you let him leave without smoothing things over?"

That's when it hits me. He was here to apologize. He brought coffee and good donuts. The good donuts from Wilsons. Even though he couldn't have possibly known they were the good donuts, somehow he did. And coffee. She's right—guilty people don't do that.

Oh god, what have I done?

"I don't know," I cry. I fling myself back onto my bed. "Now what do I do?"

"Now you apologize, you dope."

"Why do I do these things to myself?" I whine.

"I don't know," Tess says. "But you definitely have a knack for making things harder on yourself than they ever need to be."

"It was a rhetorical question, Tess," I groan.

"You know, I've never understood the reason for rhetorical questions. I mean, why ask it if you don't want an answer anyway? It makes no sense to me."

"How am I supposed to apologize? I don't even have his number. Ohmigod, I still don't even have his last name!"

"You said the WCWA sent out an email about him. Find it."

See why Tess is my person? When I'm frantic, she's calm. If I'm yin, she's yang. If I can't come up with the answer, she will. I grab my laptop and scroll through my emails, not finding the one that Barbara mentioned anywhere during her sanctimonious *you're disqualified* speech.

"I don't have it. I can't find it. They didn't send it to me. I knew this was a setup. Somehow, someway. This is why I didn't know. I'm not trying to be a paranoid conspiracy theorist here, but—" My breath comes faster, my heart racing at the idea that someone is out to get me. Not so much in a *they're going to kill me* kind of way, but more like a *they're out to sabotage me* kind of way. "Tess, this is just all too convenient to be anything but a setup."

"You're talking nonsense. No one is out to get you. There is no plot. You weren't purposefully excluded from the email."

"Oh, but I was."

"I guarantee I can come over there and find it somewhere between your inbox, junk folder, and trash bin."

She's right, she probably can. IF they ever sent it, that is. Which I'm not convinced they did. I hate that I am obsessing over this, but I can't help myself. Isn't it always easier to believe the worst than the best?

"Settle down, my little psycho," she chastises. "Take a deep breath and try to be rational about this. You know, the opposite of you."

I scoff at her inside joke. I tend to be histrionic in case you couldn't tell. Tess gave me dictionary once, and she replaced all the words that meant something close to irrational or quirky, with my name and tiny little pictures of me. Excitable, unreasonable, dramatic, nonsensical, nutty, you get the drift.

I follow her instructions and take a few deep breaths. *Breathe in the flower, blow out the candle. Breathe in the flower, blow out the candle.* "Okay, I'm good."

"Now I want you to do an internet search with his first name and the WCWA competition."

I do, and the website for the WCWA comes up with an announcement about Riggs as a last-minute judge substitution. They have a picture of him and a link to his website.

"He's vineyard consultant. Oh, and a grower," I tell Tess.

"Not a shower?" she quips.

I laugh despite myself, happy for the slight release of tension. "He showed and growed just fine," I tell her. "His last name is Daley."

"Now we're getting somewhere. Where's he from?"

I tell her the town, which turns out to be about two-and-a-half hours from where we live.

"Okay, that's not bad. Not so far that you can't go visit, but far enough that no one can do a random pop-by without notice."

"No one will be visiting or popping by," I tell her. "Nothing is going to come of this, no matter who lives where. I just need to apologize. Again. For doubting him. It's a professional courtesy. I don't want anyone in this industry with a poor impression of me."

"Well, it's way too late for that," Tess teases.

"You aren't funny."

"The audience at my improv would disagree."

"You don't do improv," I say.

"Don't I?"

And I have to stop and think about it for a moment. Because improv is something Tess would totally do. And she'd do it in secret, probably excelling at it, like she does everything else. "Do you?"

"I'll never tell," she says.

It drives me crazy when she does that. I can't keep a secret to save my life. Tess could take something as ordinary as the color of her socks to the grave.

"Why don't you just go talk to him at the competition today?" she asks.

"I'm not allowed in."

"Just because they disqualified you doesn't mean you can't go as a spectator."

"Actually, it does," I tell her. I'd left that part of the story out. Not for any good reason, just because it further cemented my embarrassment about the whole thing. But if you can't be humiliated in front of your best friend, who can you be? "Barbara said I wasn't welcome back to any of their events in the near future, if ever at all again."

"Wow, that's hard core."

"I know."

"Okay, then just go to his hotel room tonight."

"No way am I going to his hotel room again at night."

"Why not? The damage is done. What more could happen?"

She's right.

"Okay, I'll think about it," I concede.

"Good, lets figure out what you're going to wear."

"I said I'd think about it, not that it was a done deal."

"When's the last time you had sex?"

"Night before last."

"I mean before that."

"It was a while."

"Like over a year."

"So?"

"So, muscles atrophy when they aren't used regularly."

"My vagina is not going to atrophy."

"You don't know that."

"Fine, I'll go see him tonight."

"Good, now take a nap in case your up all night again. And don't forget to shave your legs. And anything else that may need some maintenance."

"I just had a wax, thank you very much."

"Well, then my job here is done." She claps her hands together, as though dusting them off. "What time is the thing over tonight?"

"Should be wrapped up by nine thirty or ten o'clock."

"Okay, I'll be at your house by seven thirty to help you pick out an outfit."

"Thank you," I soften my voice, hoping she hears the gratitude in it.

"What are friends for?" She blows me a kiss before disconnecting the call.

I curl up on my bed with my favorite pillow and am asleep in minutes.

"Please tell me you've already showered?" Tess' voice pulls me from the void of sleep, forcing my eyes to open.

"I've already showered," I say, even though I haven't.

"Oh, thank god, because I'm late, which means so are you."

I sit up slowly, "What time is it?"

"Ten after eight."

"Ohmigod, Tess! Why did you let me sleep so long? I haven't showered or shaved my legs or anything."

"Better hop to it, chickie. I'll start going through your closet."

I rush to the bathroom and do my best to hurry through a shower, only nicking my legs twice as I shave them. Curious as to why I don't just have them waxed at the same time as my lady parts. In case you're wondering, I never have an answer to that question. It's just something I continue to ponder as life passes me by.

I make it back to my bedroom in what I feel is record time, where Tess has got clothes strewn about my bed surrounding one outfit, laid out like a person, complete with accessories surrounding, and shoes on the floor.

"You want me to wear that?" I ask.

"Got a problem with it?" she returns.

"I've just never worn that combination before. Those things don't go together."

"Of course they do, look, they're together right now and they love it."

"You know what I mean."

"Morgan, just because you bought two articles of clothing at the same time, that happened to be paired in the store, does not mean they can only be worn together forever and ever."

"I know that!" I say, staring dubiously at the layout in front of me. She's laid out a mustard-colored leather skirt that rides low on my hips and extends to mid-calf. It's stitched asymmetrical even though the hem is even. It's funky, and I usually wear it with an oversized sweater and cowboy boots. Tess has it paired with a crop top sweater with three-quarter length sleeves. Which I usually wear with high-waisted pants, ensuring the crop is showing no skin. With Tess' combo, I'm showing a good two to three inches of midriff. She's got a pair of open-toed ankle boots on the floor, assorted necklaces draping the front, and a slouchy purse to go with it. The whole look is very bohemian. I'm positive I can't pull it off.

"I wear those boots with jeans," I tell her.

"And now you wear them with a skirt," she retorts.

"I usually wear one necklace at a time."

"Yet here there are four."

"I can't wear this outfit, Tess."

"You can, and you will."

We spend the next half an hour with me protesting most of what Tess wants to do to me, and her winning. I should never have doubted her though, because the result is stunning. I look like me, only better. I look like the me I always want to be but never quite make it to. My hair is curled into loose waves that tumble around my face and down my back. My makeup is barely there, yet still enough to enhance my eyes and lips. She used what felt like too much bronzer but ended up being just the right amount of shimmer on my lids and cheekbones.

It's almost the polar opposite of how she and Megan dressed me the other night, in a red retro style dress, pairing my hair and makeup accordingly, making me feel like a sexy pin-up girl. Tonight I feel like a Grecian hippy goddess.

"Can you just dress me all the time, please?" I ask.

"Happily."

I turn back and forth in the full-length mirror, marveling at how I look. Sometimes I feel like Tess missed her calling as a fashion consultant or makeup artist. Or maybe one of those stylists that actors use. Not that she isn't fantastic with computers, because she is. She writes computer code for games, the kind they use with personal gaming devices. She gets to work remotely, set her own hours, they buy her any piece of computer equipment she wants, and she makes great money. I envy her sometimes.

Most of the time.

All the time.

"Do you want me to drop you off and you can take a Lyft home?" she asks as we make our way outside.

"No, I'll take my car."

"Good luck. Have fun. You are beautiful and amazing. Any man would be lucky to have you."

"I'm not going to be had. I'm just going to apologize. That I look this good is just a bonus."

"Uh huh, okay. Call me in the morning."

My mom and grandma are sitting on the porch with their evening cocktails.

"Are you girls going out?" My mom asks.

"Gonna go drown your sorrows in men and booze?" Grandma adds with a wink.

I'd told them about being disqualified earlier in the day, when I couldn't hide it any longer since I was still at home.

"Actually, I'm going to go apologize to Riggs for the way that I acted this morning."

"He's gonna be the one who's sorry when he sees you in that outfit," my grandma says.

"You look beautiful, sweetheart," my mom says.

"Thanks guys, it's all Tess," I protest.

"Every great artist started with a beautiful canvas," Tess says.

I roll my eyes at her, yet still preen under their praise.

"Wish me luck," I say as I get into my car, closing the door and starting the engine before I can hear their responses. It would just be more compliments anyway. Any more and I'll begin to disbelieve, I'm at max capacity for my compliment quotient.

Now it's just me and my thoughts for the next twenty minutes as I make my way to the hotel. I turn up the music to try to drown them out. The last thing I need is to self-sabotage now. When I so desperately want this to be my moment to shine.

8

I avoid the valet parking when I get to the hotel. Choosing instead to self park in the main lot. Mostly because I don't want to run into anyone at the front of the hotel, namely Barbara or Michael. This way I can sneak in a side entrance. I already know Riggs' room number so I can bypass the lobby.

A well-dressed couple is waiting at the elevator bay when I walk up. The man stands behind the woman with his arms around her waist as he nuzzles her neck. The up arrow lights green and the bell dings as the doors open. The man gestures for me to step on before them. I nod in acknowledgement and make my way to the far corder of the car.

"Twelve, please," I tell the man after he picks the nine button. He selects twelve as well before stepping back beside the woman. She turns and buries her face in his chest with a sigh. He wraps his arms around her and closes his eyes as he breathes in the scent of her hair.

I feel a pang in my chest at their actions. Part wanting, part jealousy, part annoyance. I mean, I want to be in a relationship, I'm human. And obviously I'd want it to be with someone like Riggs, who I'm attracted to and enjoy spending time with and more importantly, who is attracted to me. But really, do we all need to see how happy you are together while in the elevator, for God's sake?

The car stops at the ninth floor and the woman smiles at me as they exit. I return her gesture and watch the two retreat down the hall as the doors close. My heart pounds faster, my breath becoming shallow. I turn to inspect my appearance in the mirrored wall. The difference between tonight and the other morning is drastic. Hell, the difference between tonight and the way I looked this morning when he stopped by the house is drastic.

I take a deep breath and square my shoulders, as I repeat to myself, "It's just a guy. You're here to apologize. No big deal. No reason to be nervous."

I find myself at the door to his room and slowly raise my hand to knock.

"Back for more?" a voice sounding strangely like Blondie's says from behind me. Where the hell did she come from? I turn, and sure enough there she stands, a smirk on her face.

"Weren't you already disqualified? It's not going to help to sleep with him again." Her arms cross over her chest and she tilts one hip out, foot tapping, like she's posing and waiting at the same time.

"How do you know I was disqualified?"

She waves a hand in the air. "Everyone knows by now. I made sure of it."

"Why would you do that? You don't even know me?"

"You can't just sleep your way to success. Hardworking people like Michael get cheated out of what they deserve when that happens."

"I didn't try to sleep my way to anywhere. I didn't know Riggs was a judge when I slept with him."

"Oh, please." Her eyes roll.

"Look, I don't care if you believe me or not. I know the truth and Riggs knows the truth."

"Yes, he does."

I don't like the look on her face when she says that. "What does that mean?"

"He knows you slept with him to win."

"He doesn't think that."

"Doesn't he?"

I have to wonder; does he think I slept with him to win? I didn't get that impression this morning, that's for sure. Plus, he approached me, not the other way around.

I scoff. "That's not the way it happened, and he knows it."

She looks at me, one brow cocked.

"We'll just ask him." I turn and knock on his door then step to the side, bracing myself for when he opens the door. Because once that happens, I have to see him again. And once I see him again, I have to deal with the feelings that invokes. Plus, I have to apologize for my behavior this morning. The last thing I want is Blondie sticking around for that.

I raise my hand to knock again.

"He's not there," Blondie says.

"How would you know?"

"Because he checked out after the reception started and left to go back home."

Not sure if I should believe her or not, I try knocking one more time, then step back to wait.

And wait.

"Told you," she says.

"You could have told me sooner," I tell her. She shrugs in response, noncommittal. Not that I expected anything more I suppose.

I leave, unsure what else I should do, making it to my car without running into anyone else from the competition. Though, I don't doubt that Blondie opened her big mouth and told people I was chasing after Riggs or something that would come across as equally unflattering for me.

The trip home seems to take much longer than the one to the hotel. Even though I know it's like the distance equivalent to an optical illusion, I'm still near exhausted by the time I get home. This entire experience has been taxing on my energy and emotions.

The house is dark and quiet when I walk in, my mom and grandma already having retired to their rooms. I'm tempted to reach out to Tess to let her know what happened but decide to wait until morning when I can sound more upbeat about missing him. Like it didn't really matter if I caught him or not. Like there's not this pit in my stomach that feels very much like I've missed out on something huge and important. And if I don't get it back, I'll regret it for the rest of my life.

9

TWO MONTHS LATER

By the time I let myself into the house at the end of the day, I am dog tired. Which in a way is good. Making myself exhausted any more is the only way I get through the day, or the night, without daydreaming of Riggs. Something I'm disgusted with myself over. It was one night, months ago, and still I can't get him out of my mind.

Every time I think about reaching out to him, I remember what Blondie said about him believing that I slept with him to win. I go back and forth whether or not I believe her. He didn't counter accuse me of it when I accused him of sabotaging me. But it's not like I know him well enough to know how he would respond in a situation like we had anyway.

At the time I really believed that he was trying to ruin my chances. But now that I've had time to think about it, I realize how immature that was. While I'd still like to apologize to him for my behavior, I just can't work up the nerve to do so. Instead, I just moon over him a bit, look at the pictures from Tess and Megan, and daydream about what life would be like if things were different. If I were different and didn't have him at the forefront of my mind all the time.

I even went on a date last week, a rarity that I usually celebrate when it finally occurs. All I did the entire night was compare the two. My date's brown eyes versus Riggs' green ones. The date's brown crew cut with Riggs shaggy dishwater blond. Riggs standing at six feet, two inches towering over my date at five feet ten inches if my estimations are correct. It wasn't fair to the date or to me to do it, but that didn't stop me.

So, today I was grateful for the eight plus hours of manual labor. We've got critters attacking the vines on the west side of the vineyard. And with only three acres from the start, we need every vine to be productive. And the best way to get a critter to stop eating what you don't want them to, is to give them something else. So we tried a combination of squirrel feeders, bird feeders, and no climb fencing to see which will prove most effective.

"You look tired, Sweetheart. Can I get you anything?" my mom asks.

"I think I'm just going to take a shower and go to bed."

"Okay." She pats me on the shoulder, and I turn to head down the hall toward my room. "Oh, hey, Morgan," she calls after me. "This came for you today?" she calls after me.

"What is it?"

She hands me a manilla envelope addressed to me, but with no return address notated. "I'm not sure," she says. "It came by messenger for you earlier. I didn't open it."

"Okay, thanks." I take it to my room and throw it on my bed before disappearing into my bathroom for a good half hour. That's how grimy I feel.

I dress in yoga pants and a tank top when I get out, then pour myself a glass of wine and sit on my bed to look at the contents of the envelope. I slide my finger under the lip of the sealed edge carefully to loosen the gummy adhesive. Years ago, we never would have opened mail from an unknown source because of anthrax and ricin scares. It's amazing how quickly things change.

I pour the contents out on the mattress in front of me.

The first thing I see is an invitation to this year's Wine Review Magazine's Innovation in US Wine Making Awards Ceremony.

It's a big award, I'm surprised to see I'm invited.

Second, is an ID badge with my name on it.

Makes sense, if I'm invited.

It's the next thing I see—a certificate of sorts—that makes little sense.

> *We are pleased to announce that Morgan Anderson, of Morgan's Run, is a finalist in the*
>
> *Wine Review Magazine's Annual Innovation in US Wine Making award for:*
>
> *Ginuwine Juniperfection*

Then I read it again to make sure I got it right the first time.

"Mom! Are you still awake?" I yell as I race down the hall.

"I would be now," she says. "Why are you yelling?"

"Read this, does it say what I think it says?" I thrust the certificate at her.

She takes it into the light of the kitchen and reads what it says, her lips moving as she goes, the words tumbling faintly from her mouth as her smile starts then grows to overtake her face.

"Oh, Morgan, this is wonderful news. I'm so proud of you, honey." She pulls me into her arms and kisses me on the cheek.

"Okay, so it says what I think it says, right?" I bounce in place, getting more excited by the second as it sinks in.

"What's all the fuss about?" My grandma shuffles into the room, rubbing her eyes as she walks.

"I'm a finalist in the Wine Review Magazine's Annual Innovation in US Wine Making award for Ginuwine Juniper-fection."

"Oh, honey." Tears spring to her eyes. "Your father would be so proud of you."

"He would, wouldn't he?" I ask, clearing my throat and trying to stem the emotion I feel rising in my chest. "Well, it's his vision, I'm just seeing it through."

"It's your talent that has made it happen," my mom reminds me.

"I'm going to go call Tess," I tell them, turning to skip back down the hall to my room. "I've only got a week to prepare, and she needs to make me look beautiful."

"You're already beautiful," both women say in unison. Making me smile as I shut myself in my room and grab the phone to make my call.

The Wine Review Magazine's Annual Innovation in US Wine Making award ceremony is actually a three-day event, combining conference and continuing education with a party and a pseudo-ceremony. I arrive early on day one eager to check out all the vendor booths and get my hands on the agenda so I can see which seminars I want to attend. The venue was only a four-hour drive from where we live, and I made good time having left just after the typical morning commuter traffic ends.

I check in, get my swag bag, conference info, and room key, and turn to head for the elevator bay.

"I've got this." A porter takes my suitcase and garment bag from me. "My name is Andrew. Follow me and I'll show you to your room."

"Okay," I giggle, feeling a little silly about having someone not only carry my luggage for me, but show me to my room. I don't think I have any cash to tip him. I surreptitiously check my purse for money as I trail after him. That's what you do in hotels like this, right?

"After you." He motions for me to enter the elevator before him once it's arrives.

I move to hit the button for the sixth floor.

"I've got it, ma'am." Andrew gets to it before I do.

Are we supposed to make small talk? If so, about what?

"So, Andrew is it?" I confirm.

He nods.

"Do you like the hospitality business?" I ask lamely.

"Yes, ma'am. One day is never like the other, meeting new people all the time, it's definitely not boring for sure."

I have a feeling he gave me his rote answer, but I don't know what I expected. Were we supposed to open up and have a heart to heart about our lives between floors two and six?

The elevator dings our arrival and the doors slide open soundlessly, revealing a wide corridor with plush seating and low lighting. It seems like the nicer the hotel, the more seating they have in arbitrary places. Who knows, maybe people get tired and need to sit down as they wait for the elevator at expensive hotels.

"It's a nice hotel," I say.

"Yes, ma'am," Andrew agrees.

We get to my room and he opens the door for me, then brings my luggage in and sets it up on a luggage rack, hanging my garment bag in the closet.

"Will there be anything else, ma'am?" he asks. Part of me wishes he'd stop calling me ma'am, it makes me feel old. And part of me is getting off on the fancy pomp and circumstance I'm being treated to.

"That will be all for now, Andrew." I tilt my hand in his direction, as though he should kiss the back of it, and affect a snobbish tone to my voice. An attempt at an old and English accent, as a joke.

Andrew rears his head.

I don't think he got it.

"That was a joke." I gesture to the room. "I was joking since it's so fancy and everything."

Andrew nods and moves to leave.

"You know, like old rich people?"

He keeps walking toward the door without responding.

"Don't you want a tip or something?" I ask after him.

"It's all taken care of ma'am. Have a pleasant stay." And with that, he's gone.

"How to win friends and influence people," I mumble to myself.

The room is gorgeous. The magazine paid for the cost of the room, but I'm responsible for all incidentals.

Incidentals they tempt you with outright. A small tray on a side table hosts an arrangement of glass jars. One of which is shaped like a bear and filled with gummy bears. Which makes me really want to open the jar.

Well played, fancy hotel, well played.

A small welcome basket sits on the coffee table, with a card attached.

Congratulations from the staff at Wine Review Magazine.

The basket holds a bottle of red wine, a split of champagne, which I immediately put in the mini fridge, dark chocolate, dried fruits, and a bag of assorted nuts. I grab the dried fruit to munch on, then open my suitcase to unpack.

Tess put together outfits for me for each day of the event, along with accessories and shoes with a reminder list in case I forget what goes with what. Which was smart since I rarely pair any of the items together that she did, and they would tempt me to go back to how I usually wear them. Plus, her pairings are more exciting. Like me, only better. Still my clothes, still my style, just coordinated differently.

Today's outfit being proof positive. A sheer ivory colored blouse paired with high-waisted, wide-legged black slacks and open-toed strappy heels. Usually, I only wear this blouse under something else, but with the high waist of the slacks, it takes the emphasis off the fact that it's pretty much see through, and even though my bra shows, it's not trashy looking. It feels sexy and conservative at the same time. Another testament to Tess' mastery with fashion.

I head out to the balcony and look out over the railing to gardens below my room. They are lush and green, filled with flowers, fountains, and statues, pathways winding through with cement benches for seating, and a large koi pond in the very center. The views extend to either side, the design of the balconies allowing one to take full advantage of all the beautiful scenery in three different directions.

The side walls between my neighbors and I start tall and slope low as they extend outward, giving the appearance you could almost step over them onto the next balcony. But I don't think it's that easy. I take a deep breath and sigh with content. Feeling good for the first time in a long time.

Until I hear that voice.

"Oh, god, not you again." I turn to my right to see Blondie on the balcony next to mine.

Fuck. I should have known they might be here.

"Hey, Morgan," Michael leers from beside her. "Or should I say *Maggie?*"

Deep breath, Morgan.

Don't let them get to you. This is your time, you're a finalist in an elite awards competition. Nothing is going to ruin that for you.

"Ha, you guys were right, we face the same direction and are only a room apart. I wonder who—" Riggs appears on the balcony of the room to my left, stopping mid-sentence when he sees me.

"Morgan," he breathes. "You came."

11

"Riggs," I gasp. Because never in a million years did I expect to run into him again. Let alone at this event and staying in the hotel room right next to mine. My heart beats faster and I can feel the flush working its way up my chest and face to my hairline.

"What are you doing here?" I ask at the same time that Riggs asks, "So, uh, how you doing?"

"I come every year," he says as I answer, "I'm well. You?"

"Good," he says. "Sorry, I didn't mean to interrupt, I just—"

"No, that's fine." I chuckle nervously. "I mean, you didn't. Interrupt that is."

"Good. Good." He shoves his hands in his pants pockets and looks down for a moment before glancing back up and continuing. "You look good."

"Thanks. You do too." I will my face to return to a normal shade of pale, going so far as to using my bottom lip to blow air up towards the top of my head, to no avail. "Actually, I'm glad you're here," I start.

"Yeah?" He smiles.

"Yeah." I smile back. "I wanted to apologize for how I acted that morning at my house, when you came by with coffee and donuts. I was horrible to you and I've regretted it since."

He waves me off. "It was a stressful time."

"I went to your hotel room that night to apologize, but you'd already checked out."

"You did?" His brows raise, and he looks almost boyish in his surprise.

I nod, feeling my blush creep up again. I hate that I blush. I want to be cool and calm, like Blondie, even though I can't stand her. I pivot to sneak a glance in her direction. She and Michael are both blatantly staring at Riggs and I, not even trying to hide it. I roll my eyes and turn back to Riggs. Feeling lame at having nothing more to say.

"So," I start at the same time he says, "Hey."

"Go ahead," we mimic one another and laugh. I pretend to zip my mouth shut and gesture to him to talk first.

"I know things have been weird between us," he begins. "But I was hoping to call a truce. Do you maybe want to—"

"Riggsy, I'm going down to the pool, do you . . . " A low sultry voice floats through the air, interrupting him, before settling in my direction, accompanied by the clicks of approaching high heels. Long slender fingers curl themselves around Riggs' shoulders from behind, perfectly manicured red nails at their tips. Hands that slide down his biceps, squeezing the muscles as they go, before a head peeks around the side of his then stills. The head belongs to a woman. A crazy beautiful woman with thick, glossy red hair, flawless ivory skin, big blue eyes, and plump red lips. She blinks at me, her perfect chin resting on Riggs broad shoulder, her cheek flush with his. "Oh sorry, I didn't realize there were people out here."

"Yeah, hey, Toni, this is Morgan Anderson." Riggs gestures in my direction. "Morgan, this is Antonia Alves, Toni for short."

Toni steps around him to reach over and shake my hand, giving me a glimpse of her body. A glimpse is all I need. She's in a bikini—a string bikini—and her body is amazing. I didn't think people actually wore string bikinis. I mean, I know they exist, but I kind of figured they were reserved for fictional people and movie stars.

She fills out the bikini in exactly the way I imagine it should be: full pert breasts hidden behind twin triangles of material in the front, flat stomach, small waist, identical tiny triangle between her lean thighs and rounded hips, and not an ounce of fat to be seen. She's breathtaking. And exactly the type of woman I would expect Riggs to be with.

"Nice to meet you, Morgan," she says, her smile not meeting her eyes. I'm always amazed how people can do that, smile with the bottom of their face and not the top. I can't help but let a smile take over my entire face. Even right now I'm trying hard to imitate her countenance, but I know I'm not succeeding.

"You too, Toni," I return.

"Only my friends call me Toni," she says.

"Oh! I'm sorry. Uh, Antonia?"

She nods.

"She's just giving you a hard time," Riggs interjects, smiling at me, his eyes softening.

Is that pity on his face?

Oh god, it is.

He feels sorry for me.

And why wouldn't he? My hotel room is surrounded on either side by two gorgeous couples, who are all friends, and here I am alone, not gorgeous, not a couple, no friends. I still don't even know how I was selected for this competition.

He turns to face Antonia. They are standing so close together all it would take is the smallest of nudges and they'd be lip locked. "I was just going to see—"

A million things flash through my mind in that second. He was going to see what? If I wanted to go to the pool with them and be a fatty fifth wheel? A pity invitation? No thank you.

"I think I hear my phone ringing," I lie as I back toward the sliders leading to my room. "I'll bet it's my date for tonight confirming the time. See you guys later." I run into my room and slam the sliding doors shut, locking them behind me. Then pull the curtains closed for good measure and sink to the floor cross-legged.

I should have known Riggs might be here. It's a wine industry conference. And he's in the industry. After a stealthy internet search months ago, I discovered that he is a vineyard consultant. A very good one if the articles and reviews are any sign. Which shouldn't be surprising given that he has a degree in business administration and advanced degrees in both viticulture and horticulture.

I wish I'd known that before we slept together, or fought, or whatever else we did, I would have run some ideas past him. I have a degree in viticulture and oenology, but most of my ideas come from my father's notebooks and he was self taught.

No way in hell will I ever pick his brain now. Not when "only my friends call me Toni" is around.

I bury my face in my hands, elbows resting on my knees. I just need to devise a plan to get past this and everything will be fine. I pull out my agenda for the workshops starting later today and try to figure out which ones I think Riggs might be interested in, then make a mental note to go to the opposite one.

12

As it ends up, the first thing I attend is an information session for the finalists in the competition. Where, as luck would have it, neither Riggs nor Michael is in attendance. I'm able to breathe easy and enjoy myself, and afterwards, a reviewer from the magazine invites me to dinner. Which makes me feel almost like I wasn't lying when I said I had a date.

It's not a date, it's an interview, but at least I won't be dining alone.

I take my time getting ready for dinner, selecting one of casual dresses I'd brought, a pale pink, sleeveless, pleated A-line dress, and some cute sandals that Tess lent me. I style my hair down in loose curls and add a dab of blush, some mascara, and a matching pink lipstick to my face. I feel good as I head down to the dining room, confident, pretty, professional.

The interviewer asks me to meet him in the bar portion of the restaurant, and then we'd grab a table. So that's the direction I head when I step out of the elevator. Ending up behind Riggs and *Toni,* who had stepped out of the adjacent elevator just prior. She has her hand resting lightly in the crook of his arm and from the back they both look incredible.

Riggs in a pair of black slacks and a pale blue button down with the sleeves rolled up his forearms. The top of the shirt pulls across his shoulders as he walks, accentuating the muscles there. And his ass, in those slacks. Oh, I remember grabbing those cheeks as he pounded into me. Never wanting to let go. He's got a great ass. Even when it's covered by pants.

Toni in comparison looks like a runway model. She's wearing a skintight beige three-quarter sleeve sweater dress that goes to just below her knee. A wide leather belt cinched at the waist that matches the dark brown stiletto heels on her feet. She's tall already, but the heels put her on par with Riggs. And the beige color that would make most women look like bread dough makes her look regal and gives her an even more statuesque appearance. Her hair is loose and tousled in that effortless looking way only super models seem to be able to achieve and reaches halfway down her back.

I pat my hands at my shoulder length hair. What felt sexy when I left the room now feels like I'm trying too hard. And when I glimpse myself in the wall of mirrors in the lobby, I see just how immature my dress and flat sandals are. I'm tempted to turn and head back to my room, feigning illness, when a hand grabs my elbow.

"Perfect timing," Robert, the reporter I'm meeting with, says. "And may I say, you look lovely?"

I wish his compliment would bump me out of my funk, but it doesn't. And to make matters worse, we end up in line behind Riggs and *Toni* to get into the restaurant. All I need now is Michael and Blondie to show up and my shit-tastic evening would be complete.

"So, Morgan, tell me what you're most interested in learning at the conference this year? And is this your first year attending?" The moment Robert says my name, I see Riggs' shoulders tense.

"Wow, Robert." I force myself to giggle. "You're really starting those questions early. Shouldn't we wait for, I don't know, dessert?" I try to make my voice sound like a purr, in a way I imagine Toni's voice would sound. Instead, it comes out as more of a croak.

"You okay?" Robert asks.

"So good," I say, patting him lightly on the chest. He narrows his eyes at me, can't say I blame him. The hostess takes that moment to seat Riggs and Toni, and I'm able to breathe easily once again. That is until she seats Robert and I two tables away from them and I'm left facing Riggs for the foreseeable future.

How is it possible that both couples sitting at the tables between us are situated in just a way that I have a clear line of sight to Riggs in all his glory? It doesn't take him long to catch me staring. A matter of seconds, really. And the look he gives me puzzling. Almost like he's hurt over something I've done. Which is weird given the circumstances.

I look away quickly and pretend to laugh at something Robert has said.

"Are you okay?" he asks.

"Yes, why?" I ask, smiling big.

"You seem, I don't know, off a bit? Have you been drinking?"

"Totally sober," I assure him. "Just high on life."

"Okay," he draws the word out slightly, like he doesn't believe me.

The server comes to take our drink order; I force myself to ignore Robert's raised eyebrow when I ask for a glass of Cabernet. He asks me a few more questions before we order dinner, and it feels more like we are having a conversation than an interview. I stop pretending to laugh at everything he says and faux flirting, choosing instead to focus on making sure I well think out my answers.

That doesn't stop me from glancing up at Riggs' table every thirty seconds. And every time I look, I find his hard-green eyes staring back at me.

Every. Time.

It's unsettling. And makes me feel self-conscious. At the same time, I feel protected. And how that makes sense in my mind, I'm not sure. But it does.

"Excuse me for a moment, I need to visit the restroom." Robert excuses himself from the table, making me feel conspicuous suddenly.

Riggs watches him stand and head toward the restrooms. He looks at me, then to Robert, and back to me before standing. I close my eyes and brace myself. Certain he is about to join me at my table and to say what? He and *Toni* are deliriously happy, and would I please quit staring at him all night? Or maybe that I should have joined them at the pool this afternoon since I obviously need some color to my skin?

No, he can't say that, *Toni* is just as pale as I am.

Maybe he plans to say—

The chair scooting back from the table interrupts my thoughts. It's too soon for Robert to return. So it must be Riggs.

I summon all my courage, though for what I'm still unsure, and force myself to open my eyes.

"Morgan, is it?" Toni sneers from across the table.

13

"Ton—uh—Antonia, hi." I glance around for an escape or a diversion. Something that helps me avoid having this conversation right here. Because it's the very last thing I want to do. I'd rather stand on the table and sing the final stanza of the national anthem, the part with the super high note, then talk to Toni.

And I'm not a soprano, I'm all alto. In junior high chorus participation was mandatory and while all the girls stood on one side with their frilly dresses and hair bows, I stood with all the boys on the other side, dressed in black slacks and a white shirt, with my hair in a low ponytail, so I would blend in better. Because no way was I getting my low voice anywhere near those daily sopranos, at least as far as our music teacher Miss Whitehouse was concerned.

"I'm only going to tell you this once, so listen closely." She leans over the table toward me, her eyes hard and her hair soft, with skin that is practically glowing in the soft light of the restaurant. What must it be like to have that reflection in the mirror every day? With such perfect, symmetrical features; I would never tire of looking at myself.

I sense that my jaw has dropped open in awe and force my mouth to close.

Toni looks at me with barely veiled disgust. "Leave Riggs alone."

"I, uh, I haven't talked to him in months, I swear," I stammer.

"I see the way you look at him, and I'm warning you now, fair and square, leave him alone. Don't go near him, don't talk to him, don't touch him, just stay the fuck away." She stands as she says the last part, her voice rising slightly.

The way the lights from the chandelier frame her head as I look up at her, and the shadows from the candles hit her face, she looks somehow angelic and evil at the same time. Like that moment in the Cinderella Castle at Disneyland where the witch looks normal, then lightening strikes and her face is suddenly hideous. Okay, that's a stretch, *Toni's* face could never be hideous, but still.

I see some of the other diners in my periphery, turning their heads toward us and whispering, and I immediately want to crawl under the table and die. Anything to not be the center of attention.

"Do you understand?" she demands.

"I do. No talking, no touching, stay the fuck away," I repeat in a low voice.

She nods and turns to head back to her table, head held high, not an ounce of regret anywhere in her stature. She even looks like she belongs, her beige clothes blending seamlessly with the ivory and gold accented interior of the room. She moves to take her seat at their table, a server immediately appears to assist her. She lowers her ass into the ornate chair, somehow knowing they would pull it out for her and push it back in. Because for some women that's how life works: chairs are pulled out and pushed back in, doors opened and closed, chivalry bestowed at every phase in their lives until it's commonplace.

And for a moment, besides being scared shitless of her, I feel sorry for her too. When has she had to suffer or fight? I mean, coming over here and telling me to stay away from Riggs, that was ballsy. But it bolsters me in the end, not her. That she felt the need to come over here stake her claim against me of all people, is laughable. At the same time, I'm smart enough to know that if she feels the need to do it, there's a reason for it. I've got *Toni* running scared of me.

And I like it.

14

I spend the rest of the conference dodging both *Toni* and Riggs. And, no, it's not because she warned me to stay away. How Riggs affects me is terrifying. How he makes me feel when he looks at me and our eyes meet. Like I'm spiraling out of control and I don't know how to deal with that. So, I'd rather not deal at all.

And I'm successful at it too, if you don't count the fact that I've gone through three eighteen-dollar bear shaped gummy bear containers in my room. Each time I open a jar and eat them, a new jar appears the next day. Sometimes even in the middle of the day, like magic. And I'm sure I can reuse the jars in some clever way. At least that's what I keep telling myself when I think of how over half my incidentals bills at the end of my stay will be candy.

But it's how I'm able to sustain a sugar high right now as I make my way down to the main ballroom to check out the winners of the Wine Review Magazine's Annual Innovation in US Wine Making competition. According to the agenda, they posted them about fifteen minutes ago. I had to force myself to wait the fifteen minutes to not appear too eager.

I step out of my room, letting the door close softly behind me, just as Riggs is doing the same in front of me. I debate heading in the other direction to take the stairs. Or just waiting by my door until he's on the elevator. But knowing my luck, Blondie would catch me out here. Or worse yet, Riggs would turn around and see me standing here.

So, I follow him as soundlessly as possible.

"Hi," he says as I step up behind him, not turning around.

"Hi," I return, even though I'm not totally sure he's talking to me.

"Nervous?" he asks, still not turning around.

I guess he is talking to me. "I don't think so. I've just eaten my body weight in gummy bears, so my sugar high is supplanting any other emotions trying to break through."

He laughs, then turns to face me, his jaw dropping slightly. "Wow, you look incredible!"

"Yeah?" I look down at the outfit Tess picked out for me. It's one I bought on a whim years ago, yet never wore. It looks like a short dress but is really shorts. Light beige, with sequins, three-quarter length sleeves that start puffy and then tighten around the forearms, the top is full with a low "v" and a belt around the waist with equally full shorts. The overall effect is drapey, sparkly, and sexy. We paired it with open-toed high-heel sandals with ankle straps that make my legs look a mile long.

I'll be honest, I feel like I look incredible in this outfit. Like how I felt the night I met Riggs. Which is the only reason I allow my next sentence to be so magnanimous. "I'm sure *Antonia* looks incredible in whatever she's wearing."

"She has to look good, she's a model," he says.

"Of course she is."

"What?"

"Nothing," I say. The elevator doors open, and we step inside. I'm reminded of the night we spent together, how passionate the elevator ride to his room was beforehand. And then of my "walk of shame" the next morning when I met Blondie. I still don't know her name, come to think of it.

Riggs leans against the wall across from me, with a smug smile on his face. I fidget with my purse strap and try not to stare as the scent of his cologne assaults my senses. It's not abrasive, just effective. I want to crawl inside that scent and never leave.

He looks good too. Great, though I haven't said so. He's wearing black slacks again, and really they should be an everyday staple in his wardrobe, they look that good on him. All I've ever really seen him in are black slacks and jeans. And in all fairness, both showcased all his delectable parts: thighs, dick, ass.

He catches me staring at him and winks, making me blush.

Again.

My god, how long is this elevator ride?

Has it stopped?

I glance at the floor indicator above the doors; we appear to still be moving. So to avoid continuing to look at him, I look at my feet. The polish on my right big toe is chipped. I try to curl my toe under to make it less noticeable; it doesn't work. Two large black shoes appear in my field of vision as the heat from Riggs' body invades my space.

I make the mistake of glancing up at him, his green eyes lock onto mine and don't let go, I'm helpless to look away.

"Make me a deal?" he asks.

I nod dumbly.

"When you win, save me a dance."

I nod again, then snap out of it. "Oh, it's an honor to just be nominated. I don't expect to win—"

He places a finger over my lips to silence me; I feel that touch down to my toes and back again.

"Deal?" The timbre in his voice makes shiver.

"Deal."

15

Even though the Wine Review Magazine's Annual Innovation in US Wine Making Award selection is a huge deal, the ceremony part of it is more party than anything else. They present the awards in a more off-handed way, like test scores on a bulletin board. Not literally, there is no bulletin board, instead it's a raised table with the finalists' wines lined up in a row. With the top three—first, second, and third place—on risers in the middle.

The table sits at the far end of the ballroom, so you have to walk through all the belly-up tables, past the bar, and across or around the dance floor just to get to it. And even then, it's just that—a table. Each of the bottles feature a medal, but we all know the only ones that count are bronze, silver, and gold.

A little anti-climactic in a way, which is why I approach the table with trepidation.

"Hey, congratulations," someone coming away from the table says. My heart beats faster. I want to know why they said that and don't want to know at the same time. In this moment, it could be anything. I could be a winner, in second place, third place, the person could even congratulate me because I'm a finalist.

As long as I stay away from the table it could be anything. Congratulations could mean anything. Though typically the meaning is good, right?

Go, Morgan.

Look.

I make my way closer, hands shaking, eyes downcast, daring myself to look up. Seeing how long I can go without looking up.

Do it.

I glance up, starting at the far edge of the bottle line and working my way toward the middle. Nope. Nope. Nope. The three on the left end aren't mine.

Six more to go.

I avert my eyes until I reach the far right side, then work my way toward the middle again. None of the bottles on the right are mine either.

Holy shit. That means one of the middle three is me.

I'm first, second, or third.

I close my eyes, not wanting to know yet. Trying to talk myself into believing that I'm okay with second or third. That it truly is an honor just to be nominated. That I won't feel defeated if I'm not first. Then give myself to the count of three to open them again.

One.

Two.

Three.

Open.

My breath leaves my body is a whoosh. I feel dizzy and light-headed. Like I need to take a step back and walk up to the table again to make sure what I'm seeing is real. Because I won.

Holy shit.

I won.

The smile takes over my face before I can stop it. My hand reaches out of its own accord to stroke the gold medal around my bottle.

I did it.

A sense of accomplishment with a side of euphoria sets in and takes over as I practically skip away from the table in a daze. People I've never met before stopping me every few steps to say congratulations. I feel drunk and sober at the same time. Making my way through throngs of people, all with something to say. This must be how celebrities are treated, it's got to be exhausting when it's all the time. But right now, it's exhilarating.

I make it to the other side of the room, intent on hitting up the bar, but also just needing to move my body. The energy coursing through me makes it impossible to stand still. I wish I knew (more) people here so I could celebrate with them. Have an excuse to squeal out loud and do a little jig.

Riggs is near the bar, leaning against a table with a smile on his face. My feet float on air as they bring me to him.

"I hear congratulations are in order," he says.

"I won." I smile, bouncing on my toes, not able to hold the enthusiasm that wants to burst out of me.

"You're not going to renege on our deal, are you?"

It takes me a moment to remember that I now owe him a dance. And another moment to decide I'm going to go through with it.

"Are you kidding? All I want to do is dance and twirl, maybe shout from the rooftop!" I twirl in front of him, partly for effect and partly because I can't help myself.

He smiles in return, his lips tilt up to take over his entire face, and his eyes sparkle with warmth. I want to luxuriate in the feeling that smile invokes.

"Won't Toni mind?"

"No," his brow furrows. "Why would she?"

He's right. It's just a dance. I grab his hand and lead him to the dance floor right as a slow song starts. Instead of feeling nervous, I snake my arms up his chest and around his neck as he grabs my hips and pulls me in close.

"I had a feeling you'd win this competition," he says.

"Oh yeah? Why's that?"

"Because we needed another opportunity to dance."

I look up at him and smile, letting myself get lost in his eyes. And when he leans down to kiss me, it feels like the most natural thing in the world.

Until I remember: *Toni*.

"Wait a minute, we can't do this." I step back and pull my arms to my sides.

He doesn't let go, instead spinning me so my back is to his front, then he wraps his arms around my waist and nuzzles my neck. "Why not?"

"Um . . ." My brain stops cooperating with my mouth and I can't remember what I wanted to say. My eyes search the dance floor for an answer. "Robert," I blurt.

"What about him?"

"He won't like it. Neither will Antonia."

"Robert wasn't your date the other night." Riggs breath is warm against my ear, making me shiver.

"How would you know?"

"I asked him, in the bathroom, and he said he was interviewing you."

"You what?" I spin back to face him, but he's yet to let go of me, holding me so close I have to wrench my neck to look him in the eye.

"I asked him in the bathroom, the other night in the restaurant, if he was your date. And he said no." Riggs shrugs, like it's no big deal

"You had no right to do that," I tell him.

"I wanted to know if I had any competition," he says.

"Competition for what?"

"Put your arms back around my neck and dance with me for real, and I'll tell you."

I take a moment to think about it. Not my finest moment, I'll admit. But we've already established that I can't think clearly when Riggs has me in his arms.

He raises a brow at me.

I wrap my arms around his neck and let my body melt back into him.

"I was trying to ask you out, that first day on the balcony, before you got all weird and ran back to your room yelling something about a date."

He was?

"You were?"

"I was." He lowers his mouth to my ear. "I haven't stopped thinking about you since the West Coast Wine event."

"I've thought about you too," I admit. Ashamed to be admitting such a thing to another woman's man, but doing it anyway. For some reason it just doesn't feel like we're doing anything wrong.

"And since I wasn't sure how you'd react if I called you, I figured I'd wait until I saw you here."

"How did you know I'd be here?"

"I knew you'd be a finalist."

"How?"

"Because your wine is fantastic, and when I shared it with one of the editors at Wine Review Magazine, he agreed."

"You're the reason they found my wine?" I can't help the awe that creeps into my voice.

He nods, sheepishly.

"Why? Why would you do that for me?"

"I felt bad about WCWAIC, even though I didn't have some master plot with Michael to sabotage you."

"I know," I laugh. "I'm sorry about that. But," I nibble on my lip, debating whether I should bring up what I know. "I thought you thought I slept with you to win?"

"I pursued you that night, not the other way around."

"I know, but I should have known who you were, and if I'd read the WCWA bulletin, I would have."

He shrugs.

"Plus," I continue. "Blondie told me that's what you thought."

"Who's Blondie?"

"You know, Michael's girlfriend."

"Cassie?"

"Is that her name? We were never actually introduced."

He chuckles. "Yes, that's her name. And no, I did not think that."

I relax against him once again, enjoying the feel of his body so close to mine. The sense of security that his arms around me brings. The—

Shit!

Toni!

"What about Antonia?" I ask.

"What about her?"

What about her?

"I'm not interested in breaking up someone's relationship and if you think I'd go on a date with you when—"

His lips against mine drown out anything else I was going to say as my mind falls into a Riggs fog. He pulls away after a moment, leaning his forehead against mine and groaning, "Look toward the bar."

"Huh?" I'm still in a daze after that kiss and can't remember anything about anything.

"Look toward the bar," he instructs.

I do and see Antonia sitting there, looking drop-dead gorgeous, as she gives us a wave and a smile.

"I'm confused. Did you guys break up?"

"We were never together."

"But she's in your room . . . and the bikini . . . she told me to stay away," I stammer. Something I seem to do a lot around him.

"Toni is my best friend. But that's all. We're just friends."

"Friends that stay in the same hotel room?"

"Is that a problem?" he asks.

"Yes, it's a problem! Have you seen her?"

"I have."

"She's beautiful."

"She is."

"My god, Riggs, even I would want to sleep with her if we were in the same hotel room."

"And she you," he says.

"And she . . . huh?"

"Toni likes women, not men. And call me silly, but I'd rather be with a woman that likes men, since I am one and all."

"She's gay?"

"Yup." He makes a popping sound with the p, a smug look on his face.

"I love that about her." I smile. "Wait, if you guys aren't together, why did she warn me to stay away from you?"

He sighs. "I'm sorry about that. She gets a little . . . worked up sometimes. She said she wanted to see what you were made of. I didn't know she was going to do that, or I would have asked her not to. She'd like to apologize if you'll give her the chance."

"I'd like that," I tell him, leaning my head back against his chest.

"So, does this mean you'll go out with me?" Riggs asks.

"It does."

"Can I kiss you again?" His voice is gruff.

"You can." My smile grows as he places his fingers under my chin and tilts my head up. His lips descend to capture mine and he kisses the hell out of me.

Then he does it again.

And a few more times after that too.

We stay that way for a while, lips intermittently locked, bodies fused together, swaying to our own beat regardless of the tempo in the music.

Until I'm abruptly hip checked to the side.

"Hey, Morgan, not sure if you're aware, but it's a fast song right now and you are going *slow*. I'm going to cut in. Riggs, my friend, I'll give her back in one piece. Cool?" Michael doesn't wait for an answer or apologize for barging in between us. He just grabs my hand and tugs me to the side, twirling me a time or two before pulling me into his chest and sliding his arms around my waist.

"I'm going to get us a drink, meet me at the bar," Riggs winks and walks away before I have a chance to signal with my eyes for him to save me.

"I thought it was a fast dance," I say, pushing against Michael's chest only to feel him tighten his hold.

"Doesn't mean we can't dance slow, right?" Michael quips. I want to remind him that's exactly why he just interrupted Riggs and me, but I have a feeling he already knows.

"One song," I tell him, annoyed with myself for giving in.

"I just want to celebrate your win," he says. "I'm proud of you, and a little jealous, but mostly in awe of your talent. You're really good, Morgan."

My heart melts a little bit at that. And really whose wouldn't? We finish out our song without incident and head to the bar where Riggs is ordering drinks with Antonia and Blondie/Cassie standing behind him.

Antonia takes my hand as I approach. "I'm sorry for the way I treated you," she says, her eyes soft and face sincere, making her look like a whole new person.

"Thank you, Antonia," I squeeze her hand for emphasis. "That means a lot."

"Call me Toni." She winks in return, making me flush.

Riggs turns from the bar, a glass of wine in one hand and a beer in the other. "I wasn't sure what you wanted," he says.

"The wine, please." I smile as he hands it to me, then give it a small swirl and bring the glass to my nose out of habit. "That's nice. Cab—" Something hits me hard from behind, jostling me and the wine, spilling most of it down the front of me. "Crap!"

"Oh no! Did you spill? I'm *so* sorry." Blondie/Cassie smirks, not looking at all apologetic.

I glance down to see small rivulets of wine running down my cleavage and soaking into the delicate fabric of my outfit. Everything goes white and hazy around me. I hear Riggs asking the bartender for napkins and club soda, but it sounds muted, like we're in a tunnel.

Before I have a chance to think too long on it, I toss the remaining wine in my glass at Blondie/Cassie.

"Ohmigod! What is wrong with you? You bitch!" she screeches, pawing at the front of her dress.

"Wrong? Nothing. I thought we could be twins-ies. And look? Now we are." I gesture between our matching stained chests.

Toni laughs behind me.

"Would you like to get me out of these wet clothes?" I ask Riggs.

"I would like nothing more," he says.

16

My eyes have a hard time opening. Last night's mascara holds my lashes together, making them stick like glue. I use my fingers to pry open the right, blinking rapidly to see in the dark. My head raises and my left eye mimics my right. My vision blurred and hazy. A sea of white surrounds me, accompanied by the faint smell of sex and bleach.

And man.

I slap at the other side of the bed, connecting with a solid chest as I do. An arm snakes out and pulls me into that same chest, cradling me close.

"Go back to sleep, beautiful," Riggs mumbles as he kisses the top of my head. "It's too early to wake up."

I nod and rest my cheek against the warmth of his body, letting the solid thumps of his heartbeat lull me back to sleep. Thinking of how incredible it is that one win in life can change your whole perspective—on who you are and what you deserve. And how I need to bottle this feeling, no pun intended, and keep it with me always to make sure I remember my worth regardless of the outcome.

PART I

MORGAN'S WINE GUIDE

A BEGINNERS GUIDE TO WINE:
MAKING AND TASTING

Morgan Anderson, Winemaker
Morgan's Run Winery

WINE BASICS

WHAT IS WINE?

The answer to that should be simple right? It comes in a bottle; you drink it, it's yummy, end of story. But there are some technical things that make wine . . . well, wine.

Wine is the fermented juice of grapes. Wine grapes and not table grapes. Technically, you can make wine out of any fermented fruit juice, but let's face it, there's a reason we mostly use grapes. They taste the best. Wine can be red, white, dry, sweet, still, or sparkling. And it almost always has an alcoholic content of 14% or less.

WHAT IS GOOD WINE?

There are essentially three factors involved to determine the final characteristics of wine—

- 1. The grape varietal.
- 2. The climate and soil where they grow the grapes.

- 3. The winemaker's creative aim and skill. A winemaker must be part artist and part scientist to produce something worthy of drinking.

We all have different taste buds, so in reality, it's hard for a third party to tell you what wine you should like or even what a wine *should* taste like. That said, all wines have specific characteristics which, in an ideal world, are easily identifiable. So, at the risk of contradicting myself just do this: remain confident in what you like and what you taste, regardless of what anyone else says.

RED WINE:

So, on a basic level, red wine is made from red wine grapes: Pinot Noir, Cabernet Sauvignon, Merlot. What you might not know is that the color actually comes from the skins and the seeds, not necessarily the whole grape. To make red wine "red" you ferment the grapes with the skins on. Red wines range in color from pale red to ruby to purple to inky. Red wines like to be served at room temperature.

WHITE WINE:

White wines are made from white wine grapes: Chardonnay, Pinot Grigio, Pinot Blanc. The grapes are fermented after the skins are removed. They can range in color from near clear to pale yellow to light green to deep gold. White wines like to be chilled, but not too cold or you'll inhibit the flavor

ROSÉ WINE:

Rosés are easily identified by their pink hue. They are made from the red grape and are left in contact with the skin for a short amount of time. Rosé is also referred to as Blush wine.

APÉRITIFS:

An apéritif wine has been flavored with herbs or spices to give it a unique flavor. (Like what I do.)

FORTIFIED/DESSERT:

A fortified wine's alcohol content has been increased—to 17%-21%—by the addition of brandy or a neutral spirit. Think: Port, Sherry, Madeira. Designed to be drank after dinner, or with dessert, or even as dessert. But I drink it when I want to, because it's sweet, like me.

SPARKLING/CHAMPAGNE:

Sparkling wine has bubbles. Champagne has bubbles. They are not the same. Champagne is made in the Champagne region of France. Sparkling wine is made everywhere else.

STORING WINE:

Keep it dark and away from direct sunlight. Store bottles on their side so the cork stay moist. (I know, it sounds dirty when I say it that way.) Make sure it's a cooler environment, between 50 and 60 degrees if possible. And no dry heat, a little humidity is good.

- In California and Washington, a wine need only contain 75% of a varietal to be named after it.
- In Oregon, a wine need only contain 90% of a varietal to be named after it. The exception being Cabernet Sauvignon, which can be 75%.
- In Australia and most of Europe, a wine need only contain 85% varietal to be named after it.
- Most European wines are named for their region (i.e. Bordeaux).
- Most US wines are named for their grape varietal (i.e. Cabernet Sauvignon).
- In Europe, the term *table wine* is used to describe a wine that not from a specific area.
- In the US, the term *table wine* is used to describe a wine of lower quality or distinction.
- Port is always from Portugal, but can be made from many different types of grapes. Port is usually fortified with a neutral spirit, giving it a higher alcohol content that other wines.
- When wine is fermented without the skin, it remains white regardless of the grape variety.

WINE TASTING

I know what you're thinking—why do I need to taste it when I can just drink it? And I get it, I do. But every so often you're going to run into those people who use fancy words for ordinary things and you're going to want to hold your own in a conversation, this will help. Plus, we'll totally get into drinking in the next section.

1. Check the color and the clarity. (Like with a diamond!)

- Tilt the glass slightly away from you.
- Look from the rim of the glass to the middle.
- Hold it up to a white background to see how it changes.
- For red wine is it: maroon, purple, ruby, garnet, brownish, blush, burgundy?
- For white wine is it: clear, yellow, amber, golden, light brown, greenish?

- Is the wine: dark, opaque, translucent, dull, cloudy, clear?
- Can you see sediment?

2. Smell your wine. To get a good whiff, swirl your glass for ten-seconds or so, then take a quick sniff to get an initial impression.

- What do you smell?

Swirling the wine helps to release the natural aroma by vaporizing the alcohol. Now, stick your nose deep into the glass and inhale through your nose. (When swirling, make sure to swirl and smell in one continuous motion. If you swirl, pause, then sniff you defeat the purpose.)

- What do you smell the second time around? Oak, berry, flower, vanilla, citrus?

3. Lather, rinse, repeat.

4. Take a sip. (Finally!) Let it roll around in your mouth, touching all the taste buds, and get a real feel for what it has to offer. There are two schools of thought on how to get the most out of your taste:

1. Swish the wine in your mouth, like mouthwash.

2. Suck air into your mouth, while the wine is in it, and let it aerate the wine.

5. On a basic level, you can define the flavor of wine by the balance of fruit, acid, and tannins.

- Fruit - encompasses all he tastes and smells that are not sour (acid) or bitter (tannin). Every grape varietal and style of wine exhibits different fruit.
- Acid - it's the tart taste in wine. When there is too much acid, the wine can taste sour.
- Tannin - responsible for the bitter, astringent taste in wine. Tannins are found primarily in the skins and seeds of the grape, as well as the stems. (Though, we winemakers try not to have too many stems in our wine.) Because white wines have little to no contact with these parts of the grape, they have little to no tannins.

WINE SMELLING

WHAT ABOUT THE NOSE?

Depending on how a wine develops, the nose can be nonexistent, weak, moderate, or intense. Wines that have a variety of flavors and smells are referred to as *complex*. When that variety is in harmony, it's called *balanced*. But if one thing dominates over the others, it's considered *unbalanced*.

COMMON SCENTS IN WHITE WINE:

- Grapefruit
- Citrus
- Melon
- Honey
- Cut Grass
- Apple
- Tropical Fruit
- Honeysuckle
- Floral

COMMON SCENTS IN RED WHITE:

- Berries
- Plum
- Tar
- Spice
- Tobacco
- Farmyard
- Earth
- Pepper (Black and White)
- Cherry

WHAT YOU DON'T WANT:

Certain smells MAY be an indication something is off with the wine:

- Sulphur Dioxide - just struck match. Most wine contains some sulphur dioxide (sulfites), which will be noted on the label. What you are looking for here is an overwhelming smell that does not dissipate when you aerate the wine.
- Hydrogen Sulphide - rotten eggs.
- Ethyl Acetate - nail polish remover.
- Volatile Acidity - strong vinegar
- Smells of Decay - dead leaves, vomit, wilted lettuce
- Corky - just like it sounds.

WINE PAIRING

Keep in mind that some foods and wines just aren't compatible, no matter what. The wrong wine with the wrong food can make them both taste awful. Think: chocolate ice cream covered in mustard. That said, when pairing, try to decide if you like wines that have similar characteristics with the food, or if you are more of an opposites attract kind of person.

Whichever you decide there are a few characteristics to keep in mind:

- COMPONENTS: Bitter, hot, acidic, sweet, sour, smooth, etc.
- FLAVORS: Vanilla, caramel, citrus, leather, tobacco, cherry, apple, etc.
- TEXTURE: Viscous, thin, velvety, fat, etc.

And a few rules of thumb:

- Acidic wines go well with acidic and salty foods. But, acidic foods can ruin a low acidic wine.
- Salty foods go well with sweet wines, but NOT with high-alcohol wines.
- Sweet wine and sweet food go well together, but sweet wine with spicy food is better. Trust me.
- Nobody likes bitter food with bitter wine.
- Red with meat and white with fish is a fine standard to abide by. But remember some reds can go with fish. My personal favorite is Pinot Noir with salmon.
- Italians wines will usually go well with pasta and red sauce.
- Remember the body you are dealing with. Light bodied wines work better with lighter foods and vice-versa.
- Sauce changes everything.
- There are no rules, even though we call them rules. They're just tips. The most important thing is to savor both your wine and your food. Enjoy them both.

WINE MAKING

1. Plant the vines - you can start with seeds if you want, but it takes longer. Like twice as long. My recommendation is to start with vine cuttings. It's what most people do anyway. Which is funny if you think on it too long, it becomes a 'what came first, the chicken or the egg?' As it is, starting with vines will take three years before you can yield anything of merit. Starting with seeds, closer to seven years. And really, who has that kind of time?

2. Grow the vines - don't let anyone fool you, it's farm work. Like real farm work. You have to tend and prune, water and fertilize, nurture and coddle; and still some will die. Not to mention, you have to watch for small animals who like to munch on them, then there's the birds that peck on the grapes, and of course the bees, wasps, snakes, spiders who just like to hang out around them. Grape growing is not for the faint of heart.

3. Tend the vines - more of the same. For two to three years. Blood, sweat, tears, money, energy, time, effort, water, sunlight. All the things go into the tending of the vine, getting it ready for that one special time. The first time you and yours vines will harvest together. Before it becomes same time next year and you do it again. You never forget your first time.

4. Pick the grapes (check the Brix) - I like my Brix between 23 and 25. Sometimes that happens during the day, sometimes the middle of the night. Regardless, all my grapes are picked by hand. First, doing three acres by hand doesn't take *that* long. Second, I think the grapes appreciate it more. I have a crew that helps me and we get through it all quickly.

5. Destem - we have a machine, it's called a crusher/destemmer. Though it does much more destemming than crushing. Grape bunches are literally shoveled or pitch-forked from a field bin into the top of the machine. A huge corkscrew tip looking thing spins horizontally, shaking the bunches apart, and ideally separating the main stem system from the individual fruit. The fruit falls out the bottom of the machine into another field bin where sorters (Read: people) go through to weed out any leaves, twigs, bugs, etc that have been left behind on the fruit.

6. Crush - In winemaking, this means a couple of different things. One, it's the process of cracking grape skins to free the juice. Which is done in part with the crusher/destemmer and in part with manual pressure: stomping. Yep, with your feet. Like that I Love Lucy episode in Italy. Traditionally, feet are cleansed in a vodka bath before they go into the grapes. But in the real world, I like to make sure they are manicured,

blemish free, and crazy clean. And even then its iffy. Because they're feet. Gross.

6.5 If making white move on to 9. Mostly because it's during the crush and the fermentation that the red wine gains its color, keeping it with the skins and seeds. With white wine, we remove those skins asap to keep the color from taking hold. Which is not to say that white wine doesn't have a fermentation process, it does, it's just minus the skins and after the press.

7. Fermentation (red wine) - basically this is just the conversion of sugar into alcohol using yeast. I once saw a diagram where a little man made of yeast ran around eating puffs of sugar then pooping alcohol. That pretty much sums it up.

8. Punch Down - during fermentation, carbon dioxide is released which forces all the skins and the seeds to the top of the juice. We use what's called a punch down to push them back to the bottom, thus rotating the juice from the bottom back up to the top.

9. Press the grapes into juice. We use what's called a basket style press. It looks like a barrel with all the horizontal slats separated just a bit. The grapes are scooped or shoveled into the press and the first juice to come out is called the free run. After that runs out, the remaining grapes are pressed to squeeze every last bit from the grapes.

Whites move on to ferment, reds move on to aging.

10. Age - age in barrel or in bottle. Malolactic fermentation - malic acid (bad) is turned to Lactic acid (good).

11. Racking (red wine) - Racking is when you transfer wine from one container to another. Usually one barrel to another or whatever container you are aging the wine in. Dead yeast and weird stuff will be left behind in the container, which is then washed out so the container can be used again.

12. Filter/Fining - Before you bottle the wine, the juice needs to be filtered and fined to make sure it's pretty. The filtering helps remove any particles that may have developed during the aging/barreling process. With fining, this sounds gross I know, but sometimes we'll add egg white to the wine before it's bottled. There's a method to the madness, I promise. It acts as a fining agent and binds to other things (read: molecules) in the wine that are unwanted, called colloids. Some winemakers use gelatin or milk casein.

13. Bottle - There are small machines where you can do this almost by hand, or big machines that are completely automated, but the end result is the same. Wine is pumped into a bottle and you cork it. Labels might be put on now, or later depending on your preference or how quick you'll go to market.

14. Sell - This is when the magic happens. Cause if you've done everything else correctly, you should have the equivalent of liquid gold in that bottle.

WINE TERMS

More Wine Terminology than you ever needed to know.

Acidity - I love acidity in wine. It makes it come alive on your tongue. We use the terms to describe the crispness or vitality of the wine. But I feel like it's so much more than that. It's like the personality of the wine. Too much and the wine is sharp/harsh. Too little and the wine is flat/boring.

(Wine) Aroma - The word aroma goes a couple different ways for me. Sometimes it feels negative, sometimes positive. With wine, it's positive, with garbage or body odor, it's negative. See the difference? While the wine world uses *aroma* I prefer scent, it just sounds sexier. Regardless, here's what you need to know about the word: a wine's aroma comes from the grape varietal. Different varietals have different scent profiles. For instance, the fruit or herb or botanical you might pick up when sniffing your wine comes from the aroma. Wines have primary aromas and secondary aromas.

Aromatized - This is pretty much the technical term for what I do with my wines. Even though I prefer to use the term infused. But, if a wine has botanicals infused, then it's considered aromatized. Think: Vermouth or an apéritif.

AVA (American Viticultural Area) - There are specific places the muckety-mucks have declared designated regions for grape-growing and wine-making in the US. They are called AVAs.

(Wine) Bouquet - The wine bouquet comes from the fermentation and aging. Different oak types for the barrel can impart different bouquets in the wine. Yeast, spice, or nut smells all come from the bouquet. Vanilla is the most common, which comes from new oak barrels.

Body - I used to think it was kind of sexist that wine has legs and a body, but mostly because I thought of all wine as being female. I've since changed my mind. Wine can be light and sexy or heavy and dominating. The body is a perfect indicator of which it is. The body of the wine is literally how it feels on your palate or in your mouth. Is it light? Medium? Full? Those are the common qualifiers for body in wine.

Breathe - Does anyone else think of the Faith Hill song? Just Breathe? Anyway, wine, like most of us, likes to breathe. And when you let it do so, you let it open up via the introduction of air. Hence, the term to breathe.

Brix - A winemaker will measure the Brix in the grapes (before harvest) to see what the alcohol content will be. You can roughly count on each gram of fermented sugar turning into about a 1/2 gram of alcohol.

Bung - I know, it's a funny name. My friend Tess works with computers and they have something called a dongle, which is almost as funny. Anyway, a bung is the big rubber stopper used in the hole of the barrel.

Cap - When the grapes are fermenting, either in a field bin (for smaller producers) or a vat, there is a layer of grape skins that are forced to the top by rising carbon dioxide gas. We do something called a punch down, frequently to push them back down to the bottom and make sure the grapes are rotating.

Cooked - You know when you spend the day in the sun and you feel baked? Wine gets the same way when exposed to high heat or extreme temperature fluctuations. When a wine is "cooked" it tastes *off* and can be reminiscent of canned or stewed fruit.

Cork taint - That smell when you give a dog a bath and they aren't all the way dry yet? That's how a wine with cork taint smells. Because the cork literally gets infected with a fungus (I know, gross) and it taints the wine.

Corked - I know what you're thinking, it's just cooked with an "r" instead of an "o" and you aren't totally wrong. But instead of a temperature fluctuation, this is caused by the cork taint.

Crush - In my twelve-step guide for making wine, step number six is Crush. The process of crushing the grapes in the crusher/destemmer is called crush. But then, just to confuse things, we also call the annual grape harvest "crush."

Decant - For the fancy times. Or when you want to remove any sediment that might be hanging out in the bottom of the bottle and aerate the wine. That's why decanters have big bottoms and narrow pour spouts. The big bottom gives as much wine surface as possible as much oxygen as possible. Unlike oxidation, this is good oxygen that the wine will benefit from.

Demi-sec - Medium dry wine.

Dry - Not sweet.

Earthy - Remember when we said the aroma comes from the grape and the terroir? Earthy describes an aroma, or flavor, of wine that has a soil-like quality. It sounds gross, but it's really tasty. Trust me.

Estate wine - The big wine label that owns the land my mom, grandma and I live on, most of their wines are estate because it's made from the grapes they grow at the same place where the winemaking facility is located.

Field Bin – Just like it sounds, it's a bin used in the field to transport grapes. Also, sometimes used to ferment grapes.

Filtration - Before you bottle the wine, the juice needs to be filtered and fined to make sure it's pretty. The filtering helps remove any particles that may have developed during the aging/barreling process.

Fining - This sounds gross, I know, but sometimes we'll add egg white to the wine before it's bottled. There's a method to the madness, I promise. It acts as a fining agent and binds to other things (read: molecules) in the wine that are unwanted, called colloids. Some winemakers use gelatin or milk casein.

Fortified wine - When a wine is fortified, we've added booze to it. A distilled spirit. Port and Sherry are good examples of fortified wines. As is Vermouth, but Vermouth is also aromatized. Hard to believe its even wine at all when it's fortified and aromatized, huh? But it is, I checked.

Free Run - Once you load the fermented grapes into the press, but before you press them, juice will run out/off - that's call free run. It's usually considered the best since the juice is from the natural breaking of the grape skin and not the mechanical breaking. Simply put, it's the juice after the crush but before the press.

Green - Like when you call someone who is new at something "green" - such is the way with wine. If a wine tastes under-ripe, we call it green. But we also call it green if there are vegetal flavors in the wine.

Hollow - He who has no soul must be hollow. I don't remember where I heard that phrase, but I like it. And it fits here since we use it for wine that doesn't have any depth or body. Or, as I like to say, any soul.

Hybrid - Some of the craziness in wine innovations includes the Frankenstein of grapes - the hybrid. It's exactly how it sounds - a cross of two or more grape varietals. And started in the late 1800's as a cure to phylloxera: the great grape killer.

Late Harvest - A type of dessert wine where the grapes are left on the vine until late in the harvest (hence the name) which allows the grapes to ripen further, giving them a higher sugar content. A dessert wine has an abundance of residual sugars, that's why it's sweet. Late harvest wines are made from grapes that are picked at the end of the wine growing season. Waiting until the end of the season allows the grapes to ripen further, resulting in a higher sugar content. The most common example of late harvest wines are dessert wines.

Lees - Fancy word for seeds, stems, and skins of the grape.

Legs - She's got legs, she knows how to use them. ZZ Top? Anyone? Just me? Okay, well, anytime you swirl your wine in a proper wineglass, the liquid that sticks to the inside of the glass and kind of drapes itself back down? That's the legs.

Magnum - My favorite - it's a 1.5 L wine bottle which is equal to two standard bottles.

Must - When you've crushed the grapes, and the juice is run out, everything that's left - the pulp, seeds, skins, and sometimes stems of the grapes are called must.

Nose - Fancy word for bouquet. Though, if you ask me, bouquet is already pretty fancy.

Oaky - Back on aromas and flavors, because we like talking about those in winemaking. When a wine is oaky it has hints of woodsy aromas and flavors. Though, we use the word oaky when talking about butter, popcorn, or toast flavors as well. Like most things in the wine world, oaky has many meanings.

Oenology - The study of wine and winemaking.

Oxidation - Remember how oxygenating the wine in the decanter was a good thing? This is when too much exposure to air or oxygen is a bad thing and the wine has spoiled or gone bad because of exposure to air.

Press - Technically , it's the process of extracting juice from solids. It's a process and a machine. The fermented grapes are loaded into the press and it squishes everything down into juice.

Pruning - I know a lot of people hate the pruning process, but I love it. After harvest you go back through the vineyard and trim back all the vines. This allows for the new growth for next harvest. I think of it like an annual cleansing of sorts. The New Year's day for the vines, if you will.

Racking - Racking is when you transfer wine from one container to another. Usually from one barrel to another or whatever container you are aging the wine in. Dead yeast and weird stuff will be left behind in the container, which is then washed out so the container can be used again.

Sediment - Ever see that weird stuff that looks like gritty backwash in your glass or the bottom of your bottle? That's sediment. Relax, it's not really backwash. It's the solids that sink to the bottom of a bottle of wine; mostly seen in aged wines. Which is why an older wine is often decanted, so the sediment stays in the decanter and not in your glass.

Single Varietal - When a wine is described as a single varietal it means that wine has not yet found its special someone to share its life with. Ha! I'm totally kidding, it means only one type of grape was used.

Split - Think baby bottle. Not literally though. A split is a small bottle, usually sparkling wine, and is 187.5 ml or one quarter of the standard bottle size.

Standard Bottle - The standard wine bottle holds 750 ml of wine.

Sulfites - It's an ugly word. Everyone hates it. People think sulfites are the devil. But they aren't. This is going to sound like a sulfite rant, so I'm going to try to rein it in if possible.

Sulfites, sulfur dioxide, or SO2 is a preservative that is found in many foods: molasses, sauerkraut, canned vegetables, most condiments, potato chips, trail mix, jams/jellies. And they naturally occur in many foods as well: black tea, eggs, vinegar, peanuts, wine, broccoli. So for all those people who think the sulfites in red wine cause their headaches? Jokes on you, unless broccoli, peanuts, and eggs do too. You're probably just drinking shitty wine.

Anyway, sulfites help preserve the wine, or really any food they are in. Wines range from about 10 ppm (parts per million) to 350 ppm—the legal US limit. Wines must label if they contain more than 10 ppm, but only in the US and Australia. Nobody else cares. And, while we're at it, you should know that while wines range in 10 ppm to 350 ppm, packaged meats, prepared soups, and frozen juices are all at over 500 ppm. French fries are over 1800 ppm, and dried fruit is over 3000 ppm.

Tank - If you don't use a barrel to age/ferment wine/juice then you use a tank. Usually stainless steel, sometimes glass. But it's big, like a vat, and in larger establishments you can crawl inside one.

Terroir - Fancy word for dirt or soil the grapes are grown in. But is also known to help impart flavor into the grapes/wine.

Varietal - Fancy word for types of wine grapes. Think: Chardonnay, Pinot Noir, Cabernet, Merlot - all are varietals of wine grapes.

Vintage - The vintage is the year that the grapes were harvested. Many people think it's the year the wine is released, but they would be wrong. Don't listen to those people, they don't know what they are talking about

Viticulture - the study of growing grapes.

Yield - When we talk about yield, we're referring to the amount of grapes harvested in a particular year. So I have 3 acres, and I plant my rows 8' apart, and my vines in each row 6' apart, which gets me about 907 vines per acre. My yield averages 5 tons per acre, or 15 tons per harvest. Typically 1 ton of grapes will get you about 2 barrels of wine, give or take. Each barrel gives you about 25 cases of wine. See why I'm still poor?

THANK YOU FOR READING!

If you enjoyed this book, please consider leaving a review. Hell, even if you didn't enjoy it please consider leaving one. That way I'll know what to change for next time.

If you want to know more about my books and new releases, join my newsletter!

SNEAK PEEK - DARIA

DARIA - TWENTY YEARS AGO

The cold seeps through every layer of clothing I have on causing my bones to ache and chilling me to the core. A small breeze dances through the air, making the fur around my hood wriggle in my periphery. Fooling me into thinking something, or someone, is there. But it's an illusion. The only thing moving is the wind. Movement is not tolerated, to move is to die.

Though lying in a snowbank waiting for dawn to break, no matter how many layers of clothing and protective gear I left home wearing this morning, feels a lot like death as well. I imagine myself lying by a fire, the warmth from the flames blasting the front side of my body, forcing me to face the other way when it gets to be too much, so the other side of me can be blasted as well. If I think on it hard enough, I can almost pretend it's true. The heat singeing my bare fingers when I hold them too close, as opposed to the icy wind that envelopes them now.

The rays from the rising sun glint off the white of the snow, making it hard to see much further than a few feet. Forcing me to recalculate move to make sure I one, have not moved, and two, remember my line of sight even if I can't see it clearly.

A faint whistle floats through the space around us. If you weren't waiting for it you might think it a snowbird or a train, maybe the sound of the wind in the bare trees. But it's none of those things. The whistle is my grandmother giving the sign, which means that it's almost over now. Soon—in a matter of hours with any luck at all—I can make my brief fire fantasy a reality. Warming my body to the point of discomfort. Until the red on my skin from the cold moves to the opposite end of the spectrum and becomes a tinge of pink from the heat.

I close my left eye, keeping my right focused straight ahead; my fingers are loose, my body is rigid. I take a deep breath in, filling my chest with air, then let it out slowly as I pull the trigger. The rifle firing echoes around me, joined by the twin sounds as my siblings mimic my movements. It is only after all sounds die away that I hear my grandmother's footsteps approaching behind me. Her thick-soled boots crunching through the thin layer of ice above last night's snow fall.

"Daria!" she barks. I take that as my cue to stand and face her. My entire body protesting when I try to move. Knees begging to buckle under my weight, my spine too stiff to bend to my will, forcing my core to take on the brunt of the task. I steel my expression to ensure she sees no hesitation. No pain. No weakness. To her, we are the soldiers and she the general.

"You did well. The only one to hit their targets. It is you I will continue to focus on. Your brothers and sisters have no gift.

You, my dear, you have the blood of the *femme fatale* running through your veins. You are like me and my mother before me. This you pass along to your own daughter one day." She grasps my shoulder with her large gloved hand and squeezes. The gesture is loving and filled with praise and I receive it accordingly because it is the most that I will get from her.

My family, the Limonovs, are not an affectionate bunch. Strong? Yes. Rich? Obscenely. Ruthless? To the core. Loyal? Until death. But a tender touch has no place amongst such esteemed traits. Not even toward an eight-year-old, like myself, who is also the youngest of my siblings to have their talents tested.

My great-grandmother was the famed Lidya Limonov, a Soviet sniper in the Red Army during World War II, credited with 309 kills. To this day, she is regarded as one of the top military snipers of all time and the most successful female sniper in history. She was given countless nicknames throughout her tenure: Dame of Death, Mistress of Mortality, Female of Fatality, Gal of the Grave. But our favorite, the one we still use in our family to refer to her as, is the original Femme Fatale.

We trudge back to the house, the snow starting to fall lightly, just enough to feel wet on my face. Walking feels good, the exertion warming my body from within. I keep pace with my grandmother as my siblings scamper about, throwing snow balls and the such. No doubt feeling relief over their lack of the gift.

Jealousy fills me when I think about how unrestrained their lives will be from here on out in comparison to mine. But when my grandmother leans down to my ear and whispers, "I'm glad it was you, my *lastachka*. You are my favorite—you are the one who most reminds me of her." She's speaking about my mother. And knowing that I'm like her makes the years of suffering ahead of me almost worth it.

From here on out, I am an executioner, first in training and then in practice. To be called upon throughout my life as my family sees fit. And, when the time comes, training my own progeny to carry on the lineage.

My name is Daria Limonov and this is my story.

Get your copy of Daria

ACKNOWLEDGMENTS

Thank you to author, Tarrah Anders, for coming up with the idea for a Girl Power collection and tirelessly putting it together and keeping it going. You are amazing!

Rachel Radner - saved my ass once again. Thank you for answering my endless questions, reading my countless my revisions, and always being available when I need you.

My Beautiful, Bad-Ass, Betas - you ladies are the best! Jaime, Susan, Gabriella, Rochelle - I truly couldn't do this without you.

Missy Borucki - I abuse your good nature and I promise to really try super hard to always be on time with my manuscripts in the future. And just so we're clear, that's a promise to try, not like a true commitment or anything. I heart you big time.

Remi-Remi-Oxen-Free - my heart, my soul, my person - thank you for your support and encouragement. For always believing in me and having my back. Love you!

BW - The best decision I ever made. Twenty years later and you still make my cheeks blush, my heart sing, and my lady parts quiver. I would be nothing without you. I love you.

ABOUT THE AUTHOR

Denise has been reading since before she could talk. And to this day, escaping into a book is her go-to activity before anything else.

She likes to write about sassy women and semi-flawed alpha-esque men (hard on the outside and just a little soft on the inside.) Denise's female characters always have strong friendships, potty mouths, and like to drink—a lot.

Denise is loyal to a fault, a bit too sarcastic, blindingly optimistic, and pretty freakin' happy with life overall. If she couldn't be a writer, she'd be a singer in a classic rock band. Right after she learned to carry a tune. She has more purses than days in the month, an obsession with colored ink pens, and a slightly unhealthy bracelet habit.

Home is in the Pacific Northwest where she lives with six special needs Siberian Huskies and a husband (BW) who has the patience and tolerance of a saint. And, lest she forget, Denise also lives with too many to count characters inside her head, who will eventually have their stories told.

For more about Denise visit her website at: www.DeniseWells.com

Or follow her on any of the social media sites below.

Loving Lexie, a steamy cowboy enemies to lovers romance

Seducing Sadie, a steamy firefighter romance

Trusting Tenley, an emotional second-chance at love romance

ANTHOLOGIES

High EX-Pectations, a romantic comedy short in the **Imperfect Date Anthology**

CAUGHT UNDER THE MISTLETOE - A Holiday Affair to Remember, a romantic comedy holiday short

STORYBOOK PUB CHRISTMAS WISHES - Mistle Oh-No, a romantic comedy holiday short

STORYBOOK PUB - Breezy Like Sunday Morning, a romantic comedy short

LIMITED RELEASES

GIRLS JUST WANNA HAVE FUNDAMENTAL RIGHTS - Charity Anthology

SEEDS OF LOVE A Charity Romance Anthology to benefit Ukraine - Charity Anthology

HOT AS F$#K SUMMER ROMANCE ANTHOLOGY - SULTRY SUMMER NIGHTS

LOCKED AND LOVED: An Isolated Romance Collection

SUMMER WITH YOU: Summer Shorts Collection

JUST A LICK Collection

LOVE LETTERS Collection

STOCKING STUFFERS Anthology

www.ingramcontent.com/pod-product-compliance
Lightning Source LLC
Chambersburg PA
CBHW070511200726